D1313589

"*Souvenirs* is an evocative, pungent novel, an intriguing reflection upon what happens when hearts and cultures collide."

Warren F. Motte, author of *Fables of the Novel* (Dalkey Archive Press)

"If you like romantic fantasy, you'll enjoy this story's mating dance between a proverbial Peace Corps coed and an African national set in the Ivory Coast. Sound bites of life and love resound in *Souvenirs.*"

Shirley Maley, author of *Love Affair with the Americas* (Day of Grace)

"A spiritual journey of love and self discovery, Ruth and Kwassi's story is moving and expansive. There's magic, mystery, and tropical heat that burns up the page. *Souvenirs* is a poetic meditation on youth, idealism, and the power to heal. A lovely first novel that resonates long after the final word."

Cari Callis, author of *Life and Death on The Dub Side of the Moon, Pink Floyd and Philosophy* (Open Court)

"When Ruth and Kwassi cross paths, the attraction is mutual and immediate, and the trajectory of their romance inevitable. As their relationship runs its course, both learn that the most enduring souvenirs are not the trinkets or treasures one bargains for, but the sensual particulars of place that etch themselves into memory and the people one meets along the way."

Grace Bauer, author of *Retreats and Recognitions* (Lost Horse Press)

"Fast moving and insightful, impossible to put down."

Kris Clark, *Tipton Conservative Newspaper* (Tipton, Iowa)

SOUVENIRS

SOUVENIRS

JULIA LAUER-CHÉENNE

Community Press
Virginia Beach, VA

Published By
COMMUNITY PRESS
239 Windbrooke Lane
Virginia Beach, VA 23462

© 2008 by Julia Lauer-Chéenne
Author Photo ©2008 Judith E. Cherry

Library Of Congress Control Number: 2007939237
ISBN 0-9797572-7-4
ISBN 978-0-9797572-7-3

Printed In The United States Of America
12 11 10 09 08 07   10 9 8 7 6 5 4 3 2 1

2008 First Edition

Visit our website at www.communitypresshome.com

à Dominique

Acknowledgments

My deep thanks to the following friends and colleagues who have traveled with me on this long journey: Warren Fine, Janet Rossbach, Willis Regier, Marly Swick, Cari Callis, Loraine Kennedy, Grace Bauer, Randall Martin; my editor, Deana Riddle; and finally my husband, Dominique Chéenne, without whom this book would never have been written.

SOUVENIRS

≷1≶

Ruth met him in the rainy season when the jungle was claustrophobic with green and mildew. One afternoon she brushed her golden hair up into a bun, grabbed an umbrella and sunglasses, and stepped out into a curtain of rain.

She strolled in the storm, pleased to escape the villa full of roommates: she was weary of dominoes, English lessons, and Martini & Rossi. When she turned a corner and sank into mud, she slid out of her sandals and continued barefoot.

She waded across puddles and walked up wooden steps onto a stucco veranda to join her friend, Leslie, a young nurse from Ohio who was playing mankala with an African. The stranger picked up all his stones and dropped them one by one into a circle of twelve holes carved into the painted board. They clattered on the hard wood, blending with the downpour.

Leslie stood up and motioned Ruth to take her place. Ruth put her sandals on the floor and shook out the rain from her umbrella as the African rose from his chair.

"Enchanté, Mademoiselle." Kwassi took Ruth's hand and raised it to his lips. Ruth murmured a greeting, and for an instant saw herself reflected in his ebony eyes.

"Well," Leslie cleared her throat. "Have fun playing." She exited, relieved at the opportunity to leave. Like most African men, Kwassi made her feel uneasy, although she couldn't explain why.

Kwassi gestured towards the mankala board on a round coffee table, and they sat down, face to face on wooden chairs.

Ruth moved a group of stones around the board as she practiced her French.

"D'où viens-tu? Comment t'appelles-tu?"

He told her he was studying for his Masters in English at the University in Abidjan. By next year he would earn his diploma and begin teaching at a high school. He had come to Bouaké to learn Western pedagogy.

"It is an honor and pleasure to train with the American Peace Corps." Kwassi switched to his favorite language and paused, contemplating his next move.

"Your English is very good. Where did you study?"

"London." He picked up the pebbles and soon captured three of Ruth's holes.

"We've only been here a month," Ruth explained, brushing back stray wisps of wavy hair. "We're still trying to adjust to the climate. And learn French."

2

"I'm sure you'll be popular with your students. You're very beautiful."

"*Merci, monsieur.*" Ruth hesitated, unsure how to proceed. Finally she raised her head and met his eyes.

"You've already taken most of my stones."

"It's a matter of strategy." Kwassi's toes tapped to the rhythm of tom-toms in the distance.

"I don't have a head for tactical games. I can't plot," she sighed.

Deep enough to drink from or drown in, Kwassi daydreamed, lost for a moment in the American's startlingly blue eyes.

Ruth blinked. She thought she saw a spider, black as coal, in Kwassi's pupils.

"Mankala is a national pastime here in the Ivory Coast. You must forgive me for taking the advantage." Kwassi's smile was disarming. "I'm afraid I'm not making a very good first impression."

"I'll be offended if you let me win out of duty, or even worse, pity. Besides, there are other games, other ways to win." What did she care about tossing stones in a board full of holes anyway?

"This is true. Acquiescence should not be confused with defeat."

They turned their attention back to mankala. The game ended shortly with Kwassi's victory.

...

When the rain let up, Ruth and Kwassi walked into town on gooey red earth to the open-air market. They weaved their way through crowded, wooden stalls of fruits, vegetables, pots and pans, ebony masks, ivory, bronze, leather, and bolts of cloth. Ruth stopped at the bead vendor and stood mesmerized, scooping up glass stones that ran through her fingers like colored water.

"Beautiful! Look at the patterns—crimson, amber, cobalt blue! So many!" Ruth spread the jewelry out on the ground to have a better look. Should she choose randomly or coordinate the colors and designs? It took a long time to decide—she wanted them all! But finally she made a selection and began to bargain.

"Combien?"

The wrinkled vendor perched on top of a stool behind his wooden table, his eyes as hard as the beads at his feet. He stared at Ruth's straw bag and refused to lower his price.

"Why won't he deal?" Ruth asked Kwassi impatiently after several minutes.

"He knows you."

"No, he doesn't. How can he?"

"He knows your kind."

Ruth shrugged and wandered off to look at ivory carvings. Pretty beads were plentiful in the Ivory Coast; she'd find another vendor. Kwassi stayed at the table.

"My Brother, please reconsider your price," he said in Djoula, the Muslim's market language, tossing a bead up and down in his palm.

"My Friend, I must eat too. Twenty-five francs is not an unreasonable price."

"Fifteen. Look. There's a little chip in this one."

"That is nothing. In fact, it enhances the value. These are

old stones, from my father's people. Surely you appreciate the magic of the ancients. Twenty francs. You can afford that."

"Dear Brother, seventeen if you insist. This is a fair price even for such precious stones."

"You'll need more than this for that fair one!" The vendor laughed as he got out a fine leather strap to string the beads. "Eighteen and it's a deal. You will be deeply loved by whoever wears them in your favor."

Kwassi smiled and got out his money.

...

On the way home the sun slid out from clouds and the world blurred with evaporation. Ruth wore the market beads around her neck, touched by Kwassi's kindness. They stepped around large puddles, wandered past clay huts, stucco villas, palm trees, and children. Vendors here and there sold peanuts, fruit, watches, and batteries.

"Two francs, two francs," an African woman dressed in an orange boubou motioned Ruth and Kwassi over to her mango stand.

"Two francs?" Kwassi laughed. "Two mangoes for two francs then." The woman winked. Kwassi grinned and gave her two coins.

"Two for the price of one. I'm impressed." Ruth commented, dropping hers into her bag.

She watched Kwassi eat, transfixed by widely spaced teeth tearing into tender, yellow skin, powerful lips sucking out sweet juice. He held out the dripping fruit to her, and Ruth tentatively took a bite.

When they stopped in front of Ruth's black iron gate he

asked her to go dancing.

"I'll take you to *Chez Abdoula.* Have you ever been?"

"I don't go out much. I'm too tired," Ruth yawned. "It's the heat."

"I'll come by for you this evening."

Ruth said good-bye, her eyes riveted on Kwassi's wide flared nostrils and the carved designs on his cheeks.

. . .

A few hours later she slipped out of the villa and met him at the corner.

At *Chez Abdoula* an orchestra under a thatched roof had Africans in a dancing frenzy. Ruth and Kwassi, the only black and white couple, were welcomed enthusiastically as the clientele whistled and clapped. Kwassi taught Ruth some steps, holding her waist and guiding her hips. She imitated as best she could, enjoying the syncopation of bongos and xylophones until she became distracted by so much color and noise. All this swirling and swaying began to make her dizzy until Kwassi's unbuttoned shirt caught her eye, his dark chest beaded with sweat. When the music became soft and romantic, they danced slowly cheek to cheek. His face was dark and rough with fine texture just the way she liked. She thought of her father so far away and felt somewhat reassured. Kwassi's fingers tangled Ruth's damp ringlets at the nape of her neck. He wanted to kiss her, but refrained. She belonged on a pedestal for all to admire. How could he possibly keep such a beauty from slipping away?

After a few more songs they left the floor and sat down on a wooden bench off to the side. Kwassi went to the bar and returned with two warm gin and tonics and a pack of Craven cigarettes. The music drowned out any attempt at conversation, so Ruth sipped her drink dutifully, longing for ice cubes. She thought hard about a question and how to formulate it in French.

"Pourquoi les noirs dansent-ils mieux que les blancs?"

Kwassi did not try to hide his glee; this ridiculous question was so typical of Americans, always trying to be sincere. How could they be so stupid? Of course black people danced better than white people. But why? This would take a lifetime to explain.

"Dancing is the poor man's recreation," he replied, using the opportunity to move closer to Ruth. "Dancing is also a mystical expression of our religion," he whispered in her ear.

"My father's a clergyman," she retorted. "My ancestors were missionaries in Africa. I know all about religion."

Kwassi pressed closer. "That's what you think." This time he couldn't resist. His lips found hers as his hand touched her bare knee.

"Va-t-en! Va te faire foutre!" Ruth pushed him back, offended.

"That's not very Christian!" Kwassi laughed, enchanted by how expertly she swore and the surprising strength of her arms. "Don't worry, you dance better than most white people."

Ruth tossed her head indignantly, picked up a Craven, and waited for Kwassi to strike a match. They danced all night and left near dawn, walking Kwassi stopped and held

Ruth's face in his hands.

"*Je t'adore.*"

"You don't even know me," she scoffed. How many times had she heard this line?

"I don't have to know you. Don't you believe in love at first sight?"

"How can you love someone you don't even *know*?"

"In our culture, there are different ways of seeing, different ways of knowing. Besides, you can't escape my charms."

"What do you mean? I'm not easy to satisfy."

"Oh, my beautiful American! You'll see what I mean. I know all about love."

From then on Kwassi was her shadow. He followed her everywhere; he told everyone he adored her. Ruth hid in her room, avoided his path, and banged doors in his face. But he was faithful to his heart and would not go away.

Mamadou, a tall African engineer wearing square, black glasses, khaki trousers, and a short-sleeved shirt with a plastic pocket pen holder demonstrated technology, taking Ruth's mind away from Kwassi who sat a short distance away in the crowded lecture hall.

"As a scientist, I can tell you that we, the natives, do not need water filters," he announced with a heavy Ivorian accent. "We are our own filter, so to speak." He smiled widely and pointed to the illustration on the chalkboard. "But for you, it is essential to boil and filter water. *Always.* It has been done for you here at the training site, but soon it will be your responsibility. Boil and filter, boil and filter. Even for washing teeth!"

Fatigued and bored, Ruth's eyes wandered to Leslie who appeared enthralled by Mamadou's presentation. Back straight and head erect, she hung on each word in rapt attention. Ruth yawned, put her head down on the desk top, and closed her eyes.

...

She sat at the dining room table with Leslie, Elaine, a political science major from Texas with fair skin and freckles, and Randy, a tall, thin anthropologist from Michigan whose satirical wit and fluency in French had already earned him a certain degree of notoriety. English books and notebooks rustled in the breeze from the ceiling fan. The shutter windows were closed to hot, oppressive air.

"What is the present perfect progressive anyway?" Ruth asked, writing the words in big black letters on a flashcard.

In response, Randy clapped his hands once and paused, palms up and head cocked, the Ivorian equivalent of shrugging.

"You don't need to know to teach it," Elaine said in a Southern drawl. "In the Ivory Coast, that is."

"I need an example," Ruth stated.

A loud knock on the door interrupted their discussion. Elaine got up to peep out the window.

"Looks like Mamadou," she called from the hallway.

"I'll get it." Leslie stood up.

"Yeah, we need an example," Randy agreed, returning to the lesson plan. He, Ruth, and Elaine sat at the table and pondered blankly, shooing away flies.

"It's Kwassi." Leslie reappeared, miffed at Elaine's little joke. "What should I do?" she asked Ruth pointedly.

Ruth clapped her hands once and paused, palms up and

head cocked.

"What does he want?" Randy glanced at his watch. "Isn't it siesta time?"

"You better not let him through the door," Elaine warned. "They're all the same. Once they're in, they stay forever."

Leslie sighed and returned to the front door.

Randy slapped the table with his palm. "Sorry. A mosquito. It's been driving me crazy."

"It's been driving me crazy," Ruth repeated. "The present perfect progressive!"

"I got rid of him for now, but he says he'll be back later," Leslie announced, taking her place at the table. "I'm not answering the door again."

"Oh Leslie," Randy teased, "a little frilly apron and maid's cap would so become you. You could be our official *gardienne*."

"Yeah, Leslie. What if Mamadou *does* come for a visit?" Elaine asked.

"Shut up."

"Sorry, Leslie," Ruth said, trying to diffuse the tension. "I don't know what to say about Kwassi. I wish this place had a back door."

"You can't hide. Let him fuck you and get it over with," Leslie advised.

"I can't do *that!*"

"Yes, you can," Leslie insisted. "It's the seventies. We're liberated."

"Speak for yourself." Elaine emphatically shut her English

book. "If any of those darkies puts a finger on me, I'll throw up."

"Enough of this," Randy yawned. "It's siesta time."

"What about the lesson?" Ruth asked, doodling on her page.

"All you have to do is talk and smile," Randy told her. "The students repeat, word for word."

"Don't worry," Elaine agreed. "It really doesn't matter if they don't know what they're saying."

When Ruth finally got up the courage to leave the villa a couple of hours later, she did so furtively, looking in both directions before walking down the front steps. She thought the coast was clear, but when she reached the dirt path Kwassi suddenly appeared and took her arm.

"Give in, my little American. You can't escape."

"This isn't a mankala game," she said hotly. "I'm not some prize."

Kwassi let go of Ruth's arm and brought her hand to his lips.

"Forgive me," he pleaded. "I'm sorry if I've offended you." He caressed her fingers gently.

"I don't understand what you want." How could anyone be so obsessive, so blind to black and white?

"Please accept my apology. I promise I won't hurt you." He clasped her hand in both of his. "I'm sorry for my indiscretion. Sometimes I forget Americans' need for privacy."

"Well, OK. I guess we can be friends. If you promise to stop following me."

"Will you wear the market necklace?"

"In your honor?" Ruth teased. It didn't seem to matter what color or creed, boys were boys. Growing up in a family of four brothers had plenty of disadvantages but it had at least enabled her to acquire a few valuable insights regarding the male psyche. Saving face was of utmost importance to men and a sense of humor went far in helping women deal with them and their egos.

"In honor of the Ivory Coast. A souvenir from me to you with all my heart," Kwassi replied.

Ruth decided it was worth the truce. She didn't want to appear ungracious, or worse, racist and mean-spirited like some of the other volunteers. Most of them had joined the Peace Corps for a lark, not for any lofty, philanthropic cause. Some of them were already complaining about the meager living allowance and the dress code which discouraged wearing shorts in public. At any rate, teaching assignments were to be handed out soon, which meant she would be leaving Bouaké *and* Kwassi to set up house elsewhere.

...

Kwassi was taking no chances. The day the official letters arrived he approached Mamadou, who stood observing the Americans through the open dining hall shutters.

"We must put aside our fathers' differences and be brothers," Kwassi said in Baoulé as they shook hands.

"Yes," Mamadou agreed. "Although our tribes conflict, you and I entertain no disputes."

"Unlike our ancestors, we are modern, reasonable men."

"Yes. We are alike in many ways." Mamadou nodded his head in the direction of the volunteers. "It's a big day for the Americans. They haven't been this excited since their president resigned."

"Oh, yes, how do they call him?"

"Tricky Dick," Mamadou replied, proud of his knowledge. "Such an undignified name for the most powerful man in the world!"

"The *former* most powerful," Kwassi corrected him. "But their rapture today surpasses even that historical event. What's all the commotion about?" Kwassi feigned ignorance, waiting for Mamadou to reveal more.

"Oh this is about our politics, not theirs. They've just received official notification of posts for the year to come."

"Quite a group this year, isn't there?" Kwassi peeked in at the animated volunteers.

"Yes, indeed. Have you made your selection yet?"

"Yes, the most beautiful one," Kwassi replied.

"That one?" Mamadou pointed out Leslie.

"No, Ruth. The dancer."

"Ah yes, the one with the voice. Bold as a lion, that one, but too thin. Always on the run."

"Do you know where she's been assigned?" Kwassi inquired innocently.

"No. The Director of Education has made the decision. But these things are flexible."

"I'd like her to be close to Abidjan." Kwassi paused, then sighed deeply. "I'm afraid I'm hopelessly in love."

"I shall attend to the matter if you wish."

"I shall not forget the favor."

Kwassi and Mamadou shook hands.

"Thank you, my Brother," Kwassi said warmly. "But be careful. Don't scare her away. She's very independent."

"Don't worry. I understand. She'll never know of your design."

They clasped hands once more and embraced as brothers.

...

"Where's Béomi?" Ruth stared at the name on her paper, perplexed.

"It's a village. Near Bouaké," Mamadou offered, overhearing her question. He had stopped at her table in the dining hall, on his rounds of noisy congratulation and encouragement. "The last volunteer got sick there and had to be flown home."

"No way." Ruth declared. "I'm not going to a little village. It's too far from Abidjan."

"So what's the big deal about Abidjan?" Elaine's eyebrows rose in mock surprise.

"It's not what you think."

"You wear that necklace all the time."

"What's a string of cheap market beads?" Ruth asked nonchalantly. "It's not a diamond ring, for God's sake."

"Forget Abidjan," Randy urged. "Go north, not south. Come to Korhogo with us."

"Come to Adzopé where I live," Mamadou invited. "It's not far from Abidjan. We always have volunteers, and I can assure you they never fall ill."

"Is it small?" Ruth asked warily. "I don't want to be stuck in a hole with nothing to do."

15

"We have a new hotel with a swimming pool."

Ruth scanned the crowded, humid room, absently fingering the beads around her neck. She spotted Paul, a Vietnam vet with a crewcut, gleefully tormenting Sam, a slight, pony-tailed 21-year- old from Berkeley.

"Adzopé! With Leslie!" Paul jeered, reading Sam's letter.

"No bloody way! Not with that bitch! Gimme that!"

Paul held the letter away as Sam attempted to grab it from him. Ruth suddenly appeared and snatched the sheet out of his hands. "You'll be much happier in Béomi," she told Sam, smiling sweetly.

...

As the last week of training approached, Ruth grew reckless and bold. She stopped taking notes in lecture, skipped French classes, and taught English from hasty plans. She let down her long, wavy hair under the moon and got up with the sun.

The morning of the language proficiency exam she faced Mamadou, her interviewer, and stifled a yawn. He asked her to explain in French why she had joined the Peace Corps and what she hoped to accomplish.

She answered, groping for familiar words and simple verb tenses. She told him employment was an issue since in Wisconsin, her home state, there were few jobs for music majors such as herself. She wanted to travel and learn about the world while she was still young. Even though she had never desired to work in a school, she hoped to teach Africans something about America. Finally, she said she was single and adventurous. Mamadou nodded his plaited head and stroked his black beard.

"How will you remember us?" he wanted to know.

Ruth paused, not sure if he had used the verb, *souvenir*, "to remember" or the noun, *souvenir*, a memento. Was he asking about trinkets from the market or something more profound such as a keepsake?

"Could you repeat the question, please?"

Mamadou smiled and said she had made progress.

...

Kwassi had suddenly stopped bothering Ruth a week earlier, and she missed him. She wore the market necklace, danced in the shower, and smoked only Cravens. But he seemed to have disappeared into thin air. The last evening in Bouaké she declined Randy's invitation to go out for a celebratory drink. She wasn't in the mood for jokes, laughter, and bottles of cheap, red wine that the volunteers consumed as easily as Evian water. Instead she decided to visit all the Peace Corps villas until she found Kwassi. She would ask around and find out where he could be. But no one had seen Kwassi, and she feared he had vanished like magic.

Ruth was on her way home when she thought she saw a ghost. Then she realized it was Kwassi, almost invisible in the quiet night. Now that her search was successful, she could not think of one word to say. All she knew was that she wanted to be with him, that Kwassi had become unforgettable, like the souvenir in Mamadou's question. They walked back together in starlight and sat down on the shadowed veranda outside Leslie's window.

"I've been wrong," Kwassi whispered. "There's no hope for

us. We are as different as black and white."

"Don't leave me!" Ruth cried.

She clung to his neck, and they rolled onto the rough boards. Then his heavy darkness came down upon her, and there was nothing but night.

3

The morning of departure Ruth and Leslie went to the station at dawn. The *mille kilos*, named for its ability to transport 1,000 kilograms, was the vehicle they had chosen to take them south to Adzopé. The bus was parked among dozens of old cars and trucks, flaps of canvas rolled up over holes that were windows, rows of metal folded down into hard, narrow seats. The two women sat down on their trunks, crossed their legs, and got out their paperback novels.

Later they paid two Africans a franc to load their luggage and sat down inside to reserve two places. Gradually they were surrounded by black elbows and legs, pots and pans, fruit, and bundles of clothing. Long after the sun had melted away the early hours best for traveling, the *mille kilos* struggled to a start.

They chugged and rattled over potholes in the trail. From

time to time they stopped to pick up peasants waiting at crossroads in the jungle. Ropes were untied, belongings hoisted and secured upon the top-heavy vehicle tilting towards the ditch at an alarming angle.

The day dragged into endless hours of relentless sun. Ruth shoved her sunglasses back up her sweaty nose and squirmed, queasy from a sweet rotting smell. She missed the majestic firs, the aromatic pines, and brisk winds off Lake Michigan. Powdered with red dust, she longed for water and civilization.

In the afternoon the bus coughed to a stop by a green river near a little cluster of grass huts. Some village women scrubbed laundry in the dirty water while others cooked over outdoor fires in big, black pots.

The passengers descended and unloaded their belongings. Ropes were untied; baskets, bundles, and trunks were hoisted down. The driver took a break to smoke and eat. He would need assistance before maneuvering the bus upon the ferry, a few boards roped together on top of barrels floating by the shore. Ousaf, a young villager, offered to navigate with a tree limb.

The passengers welcomed the opportunity to purchase fried plantain, rice and sauce from the village women's kettles. When Ruth took out her camera and snapped a few pictures, the villagers shook their fists at her and screeched. She hastily apologized.

"Christ!" Leslie exclaimed. "Maybe we shouldn't live in the same town after all. You attract a lot of trouble!"

Ruth was about to comment that separate houses would

be preferable when a group of small children interrupted. Their bloated bellies ballooned over match-stick legs; their little hands stretched out to them, begging for francs.

"Scram! Go away!" Leslie cried.

Ruth hurried over to an African frying plantain and handed the woman a few coins. She scooped four orange, oily slices of the banana onto a palm leaf.

"Yuck," Leslie shriveled her nose. "How can you eat that? Village food."

"I know Peace Corps guidelines say it's a risk. But I'm starving. It's only a plant. It doesn't taste bad. Try some. Here."

"No way. It looks really greasy."

"It's palm oil."

"You'll get diarrhea."

Again and again the ferry floated away in thick, pea soup and returned, loading and unloading until Ruth and Leslie were left with the last group of travelers. Ruth handed her small change to a child just before she boarded and crossed over to Adzopé on the other side.

≥4≤

"Adzopé, population 10,000, is situated 90 kilometers north of Abidjan. One paved street, lined with palm trees, open windows and doors, leads to the general store that sells bottled drinks, canned goods, and milk products. Two shops owned by the Lebanese, smaller and more expensive, carry luxury items including cheese, jam, ice cream, and candy bars. Roadside stands sell household supplies such as big, plastic tubs for washing clothes and water filters.

"The bakery, about halfway down 'Main Street,' is a rectangular, cement building with a little square cut into the front, the African equivalent of a fast food pick-up window. Crusty, golden, French baguettes are sold here 24 hours a day. The long loaves are delicious, hot and fresh from the oven.

"Main Street becomes gravel a short distance from the 'commercial' district and ends at the open market. Peasants arrive at day break to sell vegetables and fruits in rough, *boarded stalls. By noon the market is closed and everyone goes home for siesta.*

"The rest of town is a confusing maze of dirt streets, houses, huts, and vegetation. Everything is green here, except the dirt, which is red. The electrical power is not dependable, so it's important to keep plenty of candles on hand. I haven't figured out where the schools are yet or the post office."

Voilà. A suitable family letter. Mother would make photocopies to send family members and preserve each one in a pile tied with green ribbon. Father would have news for his inquiring congregation.

In truth, however, the hot days lasted forever, making Ruth feel like a prisoner serving time. She was tired of the dingy motel room, of writing letters, of waiting and wondering about her new life. The luxury hotel was far from completion, the ground scarcely broken. Why had she ever listened to Mamadou? There was absolutely *nothing* in this town. No cinema, no swimming pool, no entertainment for single, white women. It wasn't a town, but a large village. If only she could find a house and begin teaching! Then she would feel normal.

As if reading her thoughts, Mamadou knocked on the door about an hour later with keys and addresses, offering to help Ruth and Leslie tour houses, advising them to choose soon before the French returned from summer holiday.

"Unfortunately, all the best villas have been spoken for, the ones with courtyards and privacy fences in the `French quarter.'" They had also been paid for, which he hoped Ruth and Leslie would understand shortly. Although the

23

government subsidized the rent for school teachers, this did not always mean adequate accommodations. But for a special fee he could arrange to have select properties held. He doubted the Americans would catch on soon, however, since Peace Corps volunteers were typically naïve and slow to pick up on nuances. The Americans and French were so different in this regard.

He drove Ruth and Leslie right and left, up and down, around twists and curves throughout the village and its outskirts, stopping here and there to unlock and throw open doors for their inspection. The houses were depressingly similar with gray tile floors and thin white walls. They had a small living/dining area, a bathroom, one or two bedrooms, and a kitchen equipped with a gas cooker and small refrigerator. The cheap furnishings included a dining table and chairs, sofa, and double bed. The windows were not glass, but shutters that opened inwards. Metal bars on the outside discouraged theft, a popular crime in the Ivory Coast. To Ruth, the neighborhoods seemed the same everywhere in Adzopé; the children were always dirty and playing in the streets, the mothers pregnant and chatting over open fires, the roosters crowing. Where was the colonial architecture of her art history books? The ornate fountains, tiled patios, and mosaic court yards? Ruth's heart sank deeper and deeper, heavy as a stone.

Finally Mamadou stopped in front of a high wire-mesh fence overgrown with vines. He unlocked a rusted gate into a spacious yard of orchids and bougainvilleas, flowering hibiscus, and coconut trees. Dodging leaves and branches, they followed a path up to a blue wooden door.

"A spider!" Leslie shrieked. "I almost stepped on it!"

"They're everywhere," Ruth replied.

"Not this kind. It's the biggest one I've seen yet. Huge."

"Where?" Ruth scanned the ground around her feet.

"Be careful," Mamadou cautioned, unlocking the front door. "It's probably a tarantula."

"A tarantula? No way." Leslie nervously hopped onto the front steps.

"Is it poisonous?" Ruth inquired.

"No," Mamadou assured them. "But the African tarantula brings deep sleep and melancholy to his victims. And delusion."

They entered through high, double front doors into a large, rectangular room with identical double doors at the far end. When Mamadou unlocked them, they swung open above a concrete staircase of potted plants descending into an exotic wilderness. A huge tree rose above the confusion, spreading fruited branches.

"Are those oranges? They're *green*!"

"What a mess!" Leslie turned away in disgust.

"I love it!"

"I hope you like snakes, too."

There were two square rooms on the west side of the house. On the east side was a tiny windowless kitchen with a door opening into the back yard and a bedroom with connecting bathroom. There were plenty of shuttered windows, wide and unbarred. The rough stucco walls glowed in soft pastels of yellow, blue, and lilac. For the first time Ruth felt optimistic about her future in Adzopé.

"You'll have a great time sticking to your furniture," Leslie said, prying her sweaty legs from a vinyl chair.

"Well, at least everything matches." Ruth eyed the two orange armchairs and sofa.

"Yeah, they're the same color as African dirt. You won't have to dust."

The next day Mamadou accompanied Ruth to the housing office and helped her with the papers. He gave her a key and congratulated her on her choice.

"It's a very African neighborhood, but that house has always been for whites." He said it was a most distinguished villa and that the landlord prided himself on the garden.

"He loves exotic plants. Do not be surprised if he shows up with specimens to win your favor."

That afternoon Ruth opened the doors, stuck her trunk in a corner, unpacked, and began dusting and rearranging the furniture. She didn't know how to attach her mosquito netting to the bed and decided to ask Leslie for advice. Most of the afternoon she spent on her hands and knees, scrubbing floors. Finally she stopped and sprawled out on the sofa, grimy and exhausted.

"How's it going?"

Startled, Ruth looked up at Leslie in the doorway.

"Fine. Sit down. My mother wouldn't believe me actually cleaning an entire house like this."

"Did you disinfect everything?" Leslie asked, sniffing the air.

"I used laundry soap." Ruth sat up, trying to situate herself around lumps in the plastic cushions.

"Why didn't you hire a boy to do it?"

"I don't feel like having someone I don't know in the house."

"Yeah, especially an African male."

"Although I hate cooking and cleaning."

"Maybe we could hire one together. Your place on Tuesdays, mine on Thursdays."

"We're expected to, aren't we?" Ruth stretched out her legs and scratched a mosquito bite. "Contribute to the local economy. Isn't that what they told us in training?"

"Yeah, we have status here. We're not supposed to do manual labor."

"Or give our underwear to houseboys to wash."

"Or wear shorts."

"Or jog."

"Do you run at night?"

"What else is there to do? The pool will never be finished." Ruth sighed, removed her hairpins, and shook out her hair.

"How do you like your yard so far?"

"Great. I can lock my gate, open front and back doors wide, and walk around nude without being seen."

"That won't last long. Especially if you keep jogging. Soon the whole town will know where the Toobaboo lives."

As if on cue a battered truck pulled up and stopped in front of Ruth's gate. Three Africans in tattered shorts climbed over the fence into her yard with machetes.

Leslie immediately marched out to investigate. Ruth put on her sunglasses and approached nervously, counting on

Leslie's bold command of French as well as her ability to act decisively.

"I can't understand them very well," Leslie announced after fitful attempts at communication. "I think the landlord sent them to clean up the yard. Or maybe it was Mamadou."

"Mamadou? Why?"

"He says it's dangerous. Spiders and snakes."

"But I need shade. Protection."

"Natives demolish greenery so it won't grow so fast. You better let them know now what to chop down and what to leave standing if you don't want everything massacred."

Ruth pointed to the vine-laden fence and said "*un petit peu.*" Then she pointed to the ground and the trees and the flowers, repeating *"coupez juste un petit peu"* each time. They watched and grinned with crooked, widely-spaced teeth stained brown and chipped from neglect. She stopped and looked away quickly.

"Let's go back to the house."

"I think I'll go back to the motel." Leslie walked over to the gate and halted. "Can I walk through this or do I have to climb over it again?"

Ruth took out her jailor-style key ring, unlocked and opened the gate. "Thanks for stopping and good luck house hunting."

"I think I've found a place I like on the other side of town. Near Mamadou. By the way, you better get some anti-theft bars for your windows."

"I like them open."

"You'll get screwed. The concept of private property

doesn't exist here. The country's fucked." Leslie hopped on her motorbike and disappeared down the dusty, red road. The men's strange cries followed Ruth to her front step. Were they laughing or singing? Hurriedly she closed and locked the double doors. Then she paced from room to room, spying through the latticework, willing them to disappear with all her might.

After sundown Ruth donned pink shorts, tennis shoes, and a yellow Hawkeye T-shirt, a going-away gift from her brother who was in law school. She took a deep breath as she crept from her sanctuary. On the street her instincts kicked in. She blocked out stares and jeers and began walking briskly past pushcarts, parked cars, and Ivorian mayhem. Once outside the village her feet had wings. Rice paddies, coffee plantations, and coconut groves whizzed by. Loin-clothed farmers and women with loads of wood on their heads chuckled in surprise. She could run forever under the stars, but knew well enough when to turn around. As she returned to the village she was spotted again so she broke into a sprint, hoping to escape attention. Children chased her all the way home, laughing wildly, trying to touch her.

"Life in Adzopé is settling into a predictable, if not yet comfortable, routine. I am teaching sixteen hours a week,

mornings only. The majority of my students are Ivorian males, although there are some girls and a few French. Leslie teaches the same number of hours with similar classes at the other high-school in town. We have Wednesdays and Sundays off. I'm having a few problems with my mobylette, but aside from that everything is fine."

In her family letter Ruth did not mention that after class on Saturdays she left for Abidjan and forgot everything but pleasing Kwassi.

...

The schools were wooden buildings divided into identical rooms of shutter windows and long desks with benches for two students each. There was a raised platform, a wall of chalkboard, and a teacher's desk. Teachers walked from classroom to classroom while students remained in their homeroom.

Ruth was still getting used to the routine. She entered and hopped onto the stage. Fifty students rose to attention. She gazed directly, as if matching names with faces.

"Good morning, class."

"Good morning, Miss Sawyer."

"Sit down, class." She motioned with her hands and they obeyed.

The first week Mr. N'Guessan, the school director, visited all the classrooms with a small grass whip.

"This is your English teacher, Miss Sawyer, who has come from very far, America, to teach you her native tongue," he declared in Ruth's first class. "Be grateful and treat her with respect. Remember, stupidity and slothfulness are not

31

tolerated here." He brandished the whip authoritatively and departed.

...

Ruth and Leslie met for tennis after classes at "The Country Club," a cracked court left over from an attempt, many years previous, to create some sort of social meeting place on the part of the French. All that was left was the cement slab with markings for tennis and an abandoned shack, the Club House. They pretended there was a net that divided the court.

"I saw my landlord at Mr. N'Guessan's office today," Ruth shouted, running to return Leslie's serve. "I think he wants more rent."

"Did you tell him to get lost?"

"As best I could, but he still wants to repaint the walls. I don't get it." Ruth could not keep track of who was who and who wanted what. Aside from Kwassi, all black faces looked alike to her, an hallucination due to the intense sun no doubt. She assumed that this man must be her landlord and responsible for the crew who showed up on her doorstep, inquiring about new colors. She didn't think the walls needed repainting, but they had insisted so she had given in. Why not? She loved colors, so she chose her favorites: sky blue for the living-dining area, pale lavender and peach for the two spare rooms, and for her bedroom, forest green.

"Obviously, he's just after your skin," Leslie said, sending a powerful serve to Ruth. "You'll have to tell him to go away."

The women volleyed back and forth until Ruth sent the

ball sailing out of bounds, and they decided to call it quits.
By that time the sun was burning holes in their heads.

In the afternoons Ruth usually read, napped, and after
siesta visited Leslie in her house by a swamp where they
slapped mosquitoes and drank beer. Bloated and light-
headed, they discussed their favorite topics: health, beauty,
and men.

"Have you noticed how the skin just under my eyes
is peeling off in very fine strips? It's weird." Ruth had
stopped wearing make-up completely. It seemed pointless
in weather where everything melted. Besides, she attracted
enough attention already with such fair skin and hair. Her
back had a fungus of little white dots. Leslie's scalp was
breaking out. Two years of Peace Corps service could not
be as long as it seemed.

≥6≤

Despite Mamadou's repeated assurances that Hôtel Plaisir would be completed in the year to come, Ruth believed not one word. She could hardly wait to catch a bush taxi to Abidjan for the weekend as soon as her classes were finished.

In the meantime, however, she had to deal with her mobylette which seemed intent on slowing her down, like everything else in the Ivory Coast. Sometimes it functioned perfectly but at other times not. There was no reason for this inconsistency as far as she could tell but there again, she was not mechanically inclined. Her brothers had taught her nothing about cars, lawn mowers, and power tools.

She guided the mobylette to the street and prayed for a clean start as she turned the ignition. The motor sputtered and died. She turned the hand accelerator and pushed down vigorously. *Rien.* She set the mobylette upright on the kickstand, sat down, and pedaled furiously, hoping to create a spark. There was nothing except whistles from a little group of Ivorian men outside her gate who had stopped to watch her struggle.

She walked the machine to the corner, hopped on, and began rolling down a steep, graveled hill. The motor caught, and she descended around deep ruts and ambling students as she imagined a sensational fall, spilling all the way to the bottom with little stones burrowed into her flesh.

Pavement. She followed the smooth road for a short distance and turned to climb the last, giant dirt hill to the school yard. Accelerating to maximum she reached the top without stalling, zoomed under a palm tree, and braked violently in a swirl of dust.

The students watched her straighten her sunglasses, brush dirt from her skirt, and maneuver the clumsy machine onto level ground. They wondered why she didn't drive a car like the French.

She went to the teachers' lounge, greeted her colleagues, and tried to appear busy and professional by checking her mailbox and reviewing her lesson plans. When the bell rang she hurried away to the classroom to have the hour behind her.

"I'm going to town," the children recited. The sentence sounded like a nonsensical jingle, but as long as the students spoke in unison, not out of turn, Ruth didn't mind.

"Run." Ruth cued the next verb as she gestured like a symphony conductor waving her baton.

"I'm running to town."

I'm running to Abidjan. I'm running away. The possibilities presented themselves in a split second inside Ruth's brain.

Heat rose in muggy waves, thick and stifling. She paced across the platform to catch an occasional breeze. The students below perspired in heavy, cotton uniforms. Their foreheads were beaded with tiny droplets and their noses were shiny.

She stopped drills to teach vocabulary with pictures she had drawn at home: "parakeet," "to fly a kite," "to go sailing." Their whispers became chatter. None of them would ever own a parakeet, a kite, or a sailboat.

She stopped abruptly and glared, daring them to ignore her, but the noise continued. She folded her arms, leaned against the blackboard, and controlled her blue eyes into an intimidating stare. When they were finally silent, she walked over to the desk.

"Camera," she said, taking her Kodak instamatic from her bag.

"Picture." She held up an old boyfriend's snapshot.

"I'm taking a picture." She put the camera to her eyes.

The flashbulb went off, freezing spellbound eyes forever. Then little shouting bodies ran and surrounded Miss Sawyer, crying and waving, reaching for the magic box in her hands.

≷7≷

Ruth loved the Hôtel Ivoire. Gift shops, restaurants, theater, disco, skating rink, and bowling alley flanked an exotic lawn bordering one of Abidjan's lagoons. The swimming pool was public, but only Europeans and Americans could afford the admission. Now it was an empty aqua mirror as sunbathers lounged in the lush, tropical landscape. Immaculate white-uniformed Africans freshened drinks with big ice cubes. High heels and gold jewelry sparkled on bikinied women.

Abidjan, capital of peninsulas and lagoons, combined open-air markets, African sidewalk bars, one-room restaurants, and corner nightclubs with French cafés, gourmet dining, luxurious hotels, discos, and department stores. It was a city of manicured boulevards and spacious villas, dirt streets and shanties. Home of the President's palace and the country's only university, Abidjan flaunted its riches as crown jewel of the Ivory Coast. That it was a flawed gem did not bother Ruth.

She walked to Kwassi's small apartment near the university and let herself in with the key he had given her. The low, block building contained several units of cement walls and floors. There was one bedroom with a window and a closet, one room with a folding table, chair, and book shelves. Outside, in a small courtyard, Kwassi hung his laundry over mango bushes to dry. A shower, toilet, and portable gas cooker were to the right in two small enclosures.

Nothing mattered to Ruth as long as she could be with Kwassi. After all, the bed was the main piece of furniture, and it was long, wide, and comfortable. She took an issue of *Time* magazine from his table and lay down to read about President Ford tripping over his own feet but soon drifted off to sleep.

"Mon Amour." Kwassi stood above her, a dream come true. "It's so good to see you again. How have you been?"

"I've survived my first two weeks of teaching," Ruth sleepily answered.

"I'm sure your students adore you."

"We're working on verb tenses. I don't think they get the connection between past, present, and future."

"These distinctions do not exist in our language." Kwassi slipped off his sandals, unbuttoned his shirt and lay down on the bed.

"How do you designate time?"

"Through memory and imagination." He kissed her neck, gently at first, then sucked, making a small bruise.

"Kwassi!" She pulled away and put her finger on his forehead. Slowly she drew an imaginary line down the middle of his face. "How did you get these?" She asked, tracing the long scars on his cheeks. "They look like spider legs."

"In our tribe one follows the path of the ancients. We endure rites in which blood is drawn. I am marked in the sacred totem of my fathers."

"What does that mean?"

"Pain creates even more pleasure, my little American," he murmured, pulling her close. "These things you cannot understand."

≷8≶

The Abidjan station, a dusty terrain of bush taxis and *mille kilos*, was a kaleidoscope of activity when Ruth arrived early Sunday afternoon. Vendors sold chewing gum, batteries, cigarettes, and Bic pens behind portable stands. Women promenaded with calabashes of fruit on their heads. Merchants squatted and cajoled beside blankets of ivory and ebony. Ruth walked among signs poked in the red dirt, searching for one that said Adzopé.

"Adzopé, Adzopé, Adzopé," she heard a chauffeur chanting the town into song.

"Oui, Adzopé." She gave him the money, and he told her to get in the car.

"Combien de places restent encore?"

"C'est plein." He disappeared to round up the rest of the passengers, humming and counting his money.

She slid across the middle to a window seat behind the driver. Three old African men dressed in boubous squeezed into the back, shoulder to shoulder, hip to hip. An Ivorian businessman in a short-sleeved suit sat in front with a bulky, plastic briefcase.

The door by her side opened. A tall, turbaned Muslim claimed her place. His robe was specked with dust, and he reeked of garlic. An African man in a print ensemble resembling pajamas took the other window. Ruth sighed and moved over onto the hump in the middle.

Body odors, foul breaths, and sporadic conversations swirled around her. The chauffeur stepped on the gas and they lurched forward. She watched tensely, mentally instructing him to slow down, look carefully, and not to pass on blind curves. After Abidjan they were immersed in banana groves and coffee plantations. Finally they were rushing past giant trees and thick, shadowed underbrush. Soon the sun would be gone. She hated going back to Adzopé. She missed Kwassi already. She closed her eyes and succumbed to exhaustion, gently slipping from one world into another.

My parents are moving into a new house in the Black Forest near a rushing stream. Water, trees, nature are most important. I pack and repack, worried I won't be able to find my affairs again. There are silver candlesticks wrapped in a brown paper bag that I'm afraid of losing.

Suddenly Kwassi appears. I am in a purple, lacy dress with a low neck. My dark hair has bangs and is pulled back into a slick braid. I look French.

41

"You're too cute ," Kwassi says, *holding a camera lens up to his eyes.*

I know he's enamoured and I'm terribly pleased, flattered.

Suddenly the car was sputtering, and everyone was babbling. The chauffeur slowed to a stop, got out, opened the hood, and looked inside blankly. The businessman came to his side, pointing and advising as the old men stayed in the back seat, stoic and still as statues. The Muslim went off with his straw mat to perform evening prayer rituals while the pajama man stood in the middle of the road. Ruth rubbed her eyes and yawned, reluctantly exiting her dream world. *This can't be happening.*

After some time a small car came into view and halted. The pajama man got inside and vanished. Ruth removed her travel bag from the car and took his place in the road.

The men tinkered awkwardly, their voices rising and falling in sing-song. The Muslim walked around and around the bush taxi, fingering his beard and mumbling. Ruth wondered if any of her fare would be reimbursed. A faint rumbling caught her attention. She strained her eyes. Visions of Greyhound buses passed fleetingly.

When the Peugeot slowed to a halt, the stranded travelers opened doors and piled inside without waiting for an invitation. Ruth squeezed her way into the front seat with the businessman. Turning her head sideways she saw a glob with four heads in the back. The Peugeot pulled away, leaving the old men behind.

They clattered and shook, snaking along dips and curves. Ruth swayed back and forth, jostled up and down. Her contact lenses burned. It felt like they had been on the road forever.

Without warning the driver stepped on the brakes and left rubber. Ruth braced herself against the dashboard as they screeched to a stop. The businessman opened the door and bailed out into the night.

Yao, a policeman in a beige uniform appeared at the driver's window.

"What's going on? Where is he?" he demanded in Baoulé.

"I don't know what you're talking about," the driver answered.

"Do you think I was born yesterday, Brother?" Yao scoffed. He peered inside the car, his eyes resting on Ruth. "Don't tell me you're catering to the Toobaboos these days. They're nothing but trouble!"

"Let us be," the driver pleaded. "Surely this is not worth your time and energy. Besides, this is not even your territory. What are you doing out here so far from Adzopé?"

"Watch your words," Yao cautioned. "My uncle has powers in these parts."

"Granted, my friend, and for this reason I acknowledge your privilege and rank."

Yao made them show him their identity papers, one by one. He squinted at Ruth's Peace Corps I.D. and grafted her face in his mind. Who was responsible for her kind in Adzopé? That Christian, Mamadou, most probably, always putting a finger in every stew.

When the driver finally gave Yao some folded money, he tucked the bills into his breast pocket and smiled. Identity cards were returned, and they continued on their way.

In Adzopé the Peugot driver dropped off passengers at the station and then followed Ruth's directions to her gate. After she thanked him, he pointed to her feet.

"Hide it safely," she thought she understood him say. Dutifully she dragged the businessman's heavy, abandoned briefcase through her front door.

9

Their houseboy, Kofi, had two wives and fifteen children. He worked for Leslie on Tuesdays and for Ruth on Thursdays. He scrubbed their sundresses with a big block of Marseille soap and laid them on bushes to dry. Ruth found her clean clothes on the bed, faded and stiff as sculptures. When she came home he was mopping on hands and knees, furniture piled high, foamy tides dripping out front and back doors. She walked barefoot through her rooms, savoring a dampness that was almost cold.

Ruth was beginning to feel relaxed around Kofi and other Ivorian men. She was more at ease than Leslie, she reasoned, because she had grown up surrounded by males. Yet, the unexpected made Ruth nervous and most of the time she avoided idle conversation by pretending she didn't understand French. However, this morning it was too late to hide from the billowing boubou, folds of bright fabric wrapped around a gaunt African who looked like a nomad. He was already at her front door, waiting expectantly. Ruth sighed, regretting she had not locked the gate.

"Oui?" She put on her cold, suspicious face.

"Veux-tu des grenouilles?"

She peered inside his metal pail, nodded enthusiastically, and ordered a dozen.

The frog merchant took a knife from his rope belt and knelt. He amputated the frogs one by one, using the porch step as a cutting block. He wrapped the legs in newspaper for Ruth and threw away the severed remains in her yard. They would be decomposed by sundown.

...

Yao noted the frog merchant's activities as he sat in the shade outside the Kumbali hut. Later he would visit the merchant and ask what he had seen inside the Toobaboo's house.

At the moment he was enjoying a leisurely conversation with *Madame* in her back courtyard just beyond Ruth's fence.

"Do you know your neighbor?" he casually inquired, taking a sip of palm wine. She was quite the gossip, and Yao knew she would be perfect for his little mission.

"The white woman who just moved in?"

"Yes, the Toobaboo."

"I have not yet had the privilege to meet her personally. She's always in a great hurry, moving so fast even in the heat!"

"I know her!" Moussa, her nine-year- old son, exclaimed.

The white woman next door had captured his fancy. "She has a mobylette. And a Kodak," he told Yao.

"What's that?" Yao's eyes narrowed as he learned this information.

"My cousin says she takes out little pictures from her special box. I want one."

"Have you been inside her house? Have you seen it?" Yao's voice was gentle and encouraging.

"No, *Monsieur le Commissariat*, she keeps the doors locked. But I can easily climb through her windows," Moussa offered eagerly.

"Keep an eye on her for me, will you? When you get a chance, pay her a visit."

"She is not very friendly," Moussa replied.

"We must not let that stop us. I'm looking for something I think she might have. Some important papers."

"Oh that's easy," Moussa said. "Her straw bag is full of them every morning."

"No, these are special. They look like drawings. Big pieces of paper inside a brown briefcase. If you find them for me, I'll give you a magic box."

10

There are spirits living in my house. I can feel them wandering. My affairs have been misplaced, moved. At night I hear them rustling, invisible, becoming noisier and noisier. I'm the only one who can hear them.

The clapping of hands intruded into Ruth's reverie, scattering her phantoms back into hiding with a sharp, staccato rhythm. This African way of "knocking" irritated her, especially during siesta. Who would venture out now at the sun's zenith? Stealthily she rose from her bed.

Her eyes swam until they focused on little Moussa. He was standing by the front door, bucket in hand, straining his skinny neck to glimpse inside. She quietly sank back on the sagging mattress and closed her eyes.

He had probably come for water again. She didn't know her neighbors very well. They were a typical, extended family with tom-toms and grass brooms. The mother cooked outside the hut in a big, black kettle. She pounded fou-tou, scrubbed laundry, and breast fed. The men and children came and went with the chickens that ran loose in the neighborhood.

"Madame, un peu d'eau s'il vous plaît?"

She sat up straight with a start. There was Moussa's dark head framed in the bedroom window. His soft eyes were like melted chocolate. His parched lips cracked an unsure smile.

"NON! Va-t-en! Ne me dérange pas!" She hissed her denial, shaking her head.

His eyes widened and his mouth closed. He backed away and fled over the fence, the big bucket banging. She flopped down on the sheets, settling in the stain of her perspiring body as she drifted back into drug-like slumber. A tarantula crawled along the window sill as if debating whether to enter the house.

She woke up a few hours later, groggy and irritable. Whenever she took a nap her body sank like a shipwreck to the bottom of the sea. Now she felt heavy, burdened with dreams she couldn't remember. As she wandered into the bathroom she paused, looking out at her neighbor's yard through the shutter slats. Moussa was spying again, poking his nose through her fence to get a better view. Hastily, she backed away and went into the shower. For some time a spider had been living there on her pale, stucco wall. Today his presence was particularly annoying. She held the shower nozzle and tested the water. The pressure was good for a change. Her gaze rested on the uninvited guest as she took aim.

The jet of water pried the spider from the wall. He fell near her feet and the current sucked him into the drain. Gone.

Suddenly he was back, climbing out and crawling towards her as if she were salvation. She sprayed him with water, and he was washed away again.

Legs appeared, twisted and turned, and succeeded in prying themselves up from the drain. She detached the nozzle, turned the taps on full force, and targeted, flipping him over and over until only water echoed down a black, empty hole. She turned the faucet off and reached for her towel, and shrieked. Like an indestructible mutant, the spider was climbing out again, going to his usual place on her shower wall.

Had Moussa really come to her window? Or was he part of the fantasies that consumed her like fever during the heat of the day?

The sun was low when Ruth finally decided what to do. She went to the kitchen and fetched a bucket. Back in the shower she filled it to the brim, deep as a well. She picked it up, testing the weight. Satisfied, she carried her heavy cargo across the fence to Mrs. Kumbali.

≳11≲

Ringlets of sweat dripped from her neck, her armpits, flowed like a river down her legs and back. That morning she had decided to do away with deodorant. Why bother? She was living in a sauna, her Avon stick more liquid than solid. Throwing it away had been exhilarating. Now as she looked at the students she asked herself again, why bother? For the last half-hour they had been doing drills on the past tense to no avail.

"Today I go, yesterday I —" Ruth tried the cue again.

"Went," voices here and there listlessly replied.

Ruth took an envelope and stamp from her desk. "Today I stick the stamp on the envelope," she said emphatically pantomiming. "Yesterday I —"

"Sticked," the students said.

"No. Stuck. Repeat, class. Stuck." Ruth gestured for a choral repetition.

"Stuck, stuck," they laughed, amused by the word.

"Hush! Be quiet! You must listen and repeat!" Monsieur N'Guessan liked to prowl like a panther around the school yard, noting which classrooms were too boisterous. He was probably out there again, just waiting to interrupt with that whip. Later he would want to talk to her in his office. But she knew the conversation would not be about teaching. Leslie was right; she had to avoid him at all costs. He and her landlord, Mr. Coulibaly, were in cahoots. Both were after her skin.

She waited until there was silence, then cleared her throat and began to sing "Yankee Doodle Went to Town," a different approach to grammar the students enjoyed. They had picked up the song that week, easily catching on to pitch, rhythm, and melody, natural musicians all of them, except the few French. They often danced between classes, the equivalent of shooting marbles or playing jacks. Today she wished she could teach them an historical perspective of the American Revolution to complement the tune, but she knew that was a hopeless idea.

Out of nowhere a man appeared in the doorway and beckoned to her. She nodded in return and ended the verse with "macaroni" a word that made the students explode in mirth. They had no idea what type of food this was, although she had tried to describe it to them. "It's like rice, only hollow. Like a miniature bicycle tube cut into pieces. With cheese." By the time Ruth noisily dismissed class she still had not placed the stranger's face.

He introduced himself as Adé, the businessman from the

bush taxi who had come to reclaim his briefcase. He followed Ruth home in his Renault, unaware of Yao at the roadside, hidden among students and villagers who marveled at Ruth's long, golden hair blowing like a banner behind her head. Neither did Adé see Moussa hiding in the papaya tree by Ruth's house, although his little accomplices were in plain sight hovering near her gate.

"Madame, Madame! De l'eau, de l'eau!" they cried, holding up their metal buckets.

"No water today," Ruth said firmly, unlocking her gate and wheeling her scooter inside.

"Scram!" Adé shooed them away in Baoulé. "Leave her alone!"

They sat down on their buckets to wait, humming, making a chorus, banging sticks in rhythm. The concert lasted until a few minutes later when the gate opened suddenly to reveal Adé and Ruth.

"Thank you, Miss Sawyer. You have saved my skin." Adé opened up his wallet and got out several bills for Ruth. "Please accept my gratitude."

Ruth shook her head *no* as the boys stretched out their hands, clamoring for the money. Adé told them to go home, shook hands with Ruth, and departed with his briefcase. Ruth disappeared inside the yard as Moussa shimmied half way down the tree with a papaya and jumped over the fence into his yard.

As Ruth rode past Hôtel Plaisir, the workers in shorts and
flip-flops were in siesta mode, as usual, under the palms.
Accelerating smoothly she passed a police van and buzzed
into the semi-circle drive at the post office.

A paddy-wagon zoomed into the entrance and halted,
horn blaring rudely. Yao yanked open the door and marched
up to Ruth, stomach jiggling over his Bermuda shorts. Her
bowels turned to jelly.

He shouted and waved his hands in her face. She had
entered the drive the wrong way. She fished out her Peace
Corps I.D. with trembling hands.

"*Miss Sawyer . . . Américaine . . . Toobaboo. . . .*" The
whispers became murmurs as the crowd grew and grew. He
shook her card in her eyes. She shouldn't be in the Ivory
Coast if she can't understand the rules. Where is her *permis
de conduire?* Where is her *casque?* Her face flushed as she

shook her head. She had put off completing the paperwork at the Commissariat. As for a helmet, she didn't realize it was necessary.

Yao's response was immediate, an exception to his usual lazy, delayed preference of dealing with conflict. He motioned two boys, and they loaded up the blue mobylette in his vehicle. Then he jumped into the driver's seat and wagged his finger at Ruth as his tires spun away in the rusty dirt.

"Ah, Miss Sawyer. Are you going to buy a car now like the other teachers?"

"*Madame!* I'll give you a lift. I can borrow my uncle's scooter."

Ruth forced herself to look straight ahead as if she didn't care, eyelids fluttering to hold back tears. This mini-drama was already the talk of the town. By tomorrow the students would be laughing at her.

Later her anger exploded as she and Leslie trudged along, damp and breathless in the suffocating humidity.

"That imbecile! Just because I don't have a helmet!"

"Who was he? Did you recognize him?"

"No, I don't know. Everyone looks the same in a police uniform."

"Someone stopped me, too." Leslie sympathized, raising her umbrella above her head for shade. "But I told him I couldn't find a helmet that would fit me in town, and he let me go."

"I can't communicate," Ruth lamented. "I can't think fast enough. I've got to work on my French. It must be the heat."

"Do you have a license?"

"What license?"

"You're supposed to have a little stamp on your scooter that you buy from the police. Don't you remember? Mamadou told us in training."

"No, it doesn't ring a bell. Shit. Is that what this cop meant about having a *permis*?"

"Oh, well. It's too late now."

The women paused by a roadside stand to purchase two drinks from an old, wrinkled vendor. Ruth sipped a pineapple soda while Leslie drank a bottle of water.

"How can you stand that stuff?" She asked Ruth.

"What? Fanta?"

"Don't you think it tastes weird here? Not at all like at home."

"Well, yeah. It's different. I think it's the water. This is the only soft drink I like here. I hate Fanta orange and Coke. They taste completely artificial."

"What about water? Have you figured out how to assemble your filter yet?"

"No." Ruth took the cold soda bottle and put it against her burning cheek.

"Mamadou came over yesterday and helped me with mine."

"Actually, I've been drinking straight from the faucet," Ruth confessed.

"And you're not sick? You'll turn into a village idiot!"

"Did I tell you that guy came back for his briefcase?" Ruth quickly changed the subject.

"What guy?"

"The one from the bush taxi."

"No shit? What was inside of it anyway?"

"I don't know. I never looked."

"How could you *not* look?"

Ruth finished her drink. "It was locked. He was so happy to get it back, he even offered me money."

"An Ivorian offering a Toobaboo money? Unbelievable!"

...

At the station policemen sat in front of little electric fans plugged into their desks. The ceiling fan turned a slow, humid breeze, and the large shutter windows were wide open in hopes of catching fresh air. When the women entered, Yao pulled his feet off his desk and motioned one of his colleagues to attend to them. The man shuffled to greet them behind the long counter dividing the room, blotting perspiration from his face with a colored handkerchief.

"Greetings," he said. "What can I do for you?"

"Her scooter has been confiscated," Leslie stated. "For no reason."

"That's hard to believe. Tell me how this happened."

"I was stopped at the post office. An officer took my scooter. Just like that." Ruth snapped her fingers.

"I'm sure you can find another one," the officer said, taking a clipboard from under the counter.

"It's expensive. I can't afford to buy another one."

"Fill out this form, please," he told her. "It sounds like a robbery. But I can't be responsible for that. This isn't the United States you know."

"How can it be theft? It was a police officer! I need my scooter," Ruth insisted. "How can I go to school without it? I have a job; I'm a school teacher." She took out two bills and put them on the counter. Yao smiled and took his colleague's place to face the women. He knew Americans could never recognize a black face. He may as well be wearing a mask.

"The scooter belongs to the United States," Leslie said firmly. "It's government property."

Yao took the bills and folded them into little squares and shuffled to the back storage area while the women waited. Ruth drummed her fingers on the counter. Abruptly the fans stopped. Too hot for work, the officers slowly took their feet off their desks and wandered outside in search of refreshment.

The women waited.

On his way to the bakery for bread, Mamadou stopped to slick back his hair in the police station's front window. He glimpsed the Americans inside just as Yao returned with Ruth's mobylette.

"I've seen you zipping around town. Better watch the company you keep," he heard Yao admonish Ruth. "That Adé is a criminal."

"Stop bullying the Americans," Mamadou ordered in Baoulé, suddenly appearing in the doorway.

"This is not your business," Yao said, startled but not speechless. He pointed to the motionless fans. "You've meddled more than enough. We're going to suffocate from the heat."

"Yes, I know," Mamadou retorted. "Despite your sermons,

you're as bourgeois as anyone. You wouldn't say no to air conditioning or a Mercedes-Benz."

"Watch your tongue," Yao warned. "The ground you tread is not yours."

"Let these women be. They're not tourists." Mamadou steered Ruth's mobylette towards the door. "They're professionals here to help us."

After they were out of Yao's view, Mamadou cautioned the Americans to stay away from the Commissariat. "Yao is like a poisonous spider on the wall," he declared solemnly.

≥13≤

The power failure and Mamadou's untimely arrival made Yao's blood boil, but the thought of his visit to Pathé in the tiny village of Gomon made his stomach churn. He was sure to be blamed for events that were not his doing. It was true, also, that he was considering a window air conditioner for his house, which must be kept secret from Pathé. But he could not delay their meeting, so he entered Pathé's hut with humble resignation.

"I am very sorry, Spirit Master," he addressed the old man in a loin cloth sitting on the dirt floor. "My informant tells me the map has disappeared."

"I thought you had this under control." Pathé's eyes blazed from a face carved with deep scars similar to Kwassi's. "Was it not at the Toobaboo's house? Is she not under surveillance?"

"Yes, Spirit Master, but I have been told that it has been retrieved."

"You have bungled this from the very beginning." Pathé shook his head in disgust, gold earrings glinting in the firelight. "First, you let Adé escape in the forest, now you let his briefcase vanish from under your nose. How do you account for this?"

"I beg your forgiveness, Spirit Master. We shall continue to do all we can to prevent the plans from materializing. There are other ways."

"For example?" Pathé was skeptical.

"We are not positive the electric plant is to be built on that particular plot. We might question Adé in person."

"Do not question what we already know," Pathé replied angrily. "We cannot allow construction on our sacred grounds. That capitalist Adé! He and that other Foula who so treasures Christianity."

"Mamadou, the engineer."

"They are to blame for all this trouble. They are the ones behind the foolish hotel as well."

"Yes, the Foula have joined forces with the Bureau of Culture so that the river may be harnessed. My spies say funding has been approved for these new projects."

"This is the height of insolence! The Foula have always wished to taint our great heritage, jealous of our powers. Now they are conspiring with the white people."

"It's true. More and more French and Americans arrive every month, taking away our livelihood."

"Such contamination can't continue." Pathé paused, took

his pipe and lit it in the fire. "This Toobaboo. What is her name?"

"Miss Sawyer, an American singer."

"Isn't your cousin her landlord?"

"Yes, a gardener who knows many secrets of the wild. He has assured me our totem thrives on the property."

"Continue to watch her. If it is true tarantulas nest within her ground, it won't be long before she is lulled into complacency."

≶14≷

Ruth unlocked Kwassi's apartment and put her suitcase on the concrete floor. She tiptoed, inhaling sweet, mildew air and listened. It seemed too quiet. She would have preferred spending the December holidays in Abidjan, but she had given in and finally accepted Randy's invitation. Since she had to catch a *mille kilos* from Abidjan in order to go to Korhogo, she had decided to pass the night with Kwassi and get an early start the next morning for the long trip. She had thought to continue without stopping, but she was tired. Traveling was always a nightmare and breaking up the trip into two days now seemed more logical. She opened the bedroom shutters and lay down for a siesta, convinced Kwassi would be thrilled by her unexpected visit.

There are dark, underground rivers and shimmering pools surrounded by parasols and palm trees. I am running faster and faster to find them. No more classes. No more trouble. I know the land well and love it fiercely, more than my own life. The tunnel I discover goes straight to the center of the earth. But at the end there is nothing, so I imagine a door and open it.

A key jangling in the lock broke through Ruth's dream. She took a deep breath and shut her eyes, her heart throbbing in her ears while Kwassi entered, lost in thought. He wondered if he would be strong enough to follow his uncle's commands. He had always taken his heritage for granted, but ever since this crazy love for Ruth had taken hold he had been asking himself questions. The coming days would be a test of heart and mind.

When he saw Ruth on his bed he wasn't surprised. On the contrary, somehow he had known that she would be waiting, making his decision even more painful. He bent over and kissed her forehead as her golden hair caught the last beams of light. She opened her eyes and for a moment he felt like the prince in *Sleeping Beauty*. His eyes widened into tender, serene pools then clouded. He looked away quickly to hide his tears.

"You aren't happy to see me," Ruth stated, sensing Kwassi's reluctance. Instead of elated, she suddenly felt crushed.

"On the contrary. This is quite a surprise and rather, well, inconvenient too," he said after an awkward pause.

"Why? Have you decided to leave town for the Christmas holidays after all?"

"No, I'm staying here. Muslims don't celebrate Christmas. But I will have a house guest."

"Oh. When will he arrive?"

"Actually, it's a female friend. Someone from my tribe."

His black eyes shifted away from Ruth's puzzled face. "She's still very young, but my uncle insists we get to know each other."

"I have to go now?"

"There isn't room for two of you."

"How can you do this? I thought you loved me." Ruth couldn't believe her ears. Was Elaine right about Ivorian men? Was she just a plaything, an amusing diversion in Kwassi's life?

"I do love you. But you'll be with your own people in Korhogo. With Randy. You always have a good time with him." Kwassi sighed and sat down beside Ruth.

"That's not the point," Ruth snapped. "You've deceived me."

"On the contrary. I'm telling you now. I'm not hiding anything. This is the way we live here." Kwassi took Ruth's hand in his. "We open our hearts and our homes. We have many wives and children. You know this."

Ruth snatched her hand away.

"Please don't make a scene." Kwassi swallowed hard as if the words were choking him. "This is not so different from your American free love. Aren't you a liberated woman?"

"Does that mean I screw around? Maybe I should! Maybe I will!" Suddenly the bedroom walls closed in on her like a cage. Ruth jumped from the bed, picked up her suitcase, and slammed the door shut on her way out.

In the morning invisible strings pulled Ruth from the Hôtel Ivoire back to Kwassi's neighborhood. Circling the apartment, she marked her territory: peanut vendor at corner, jewelry salesman under palm tree, vegetable market across street. She put her key in Kwassi's lock and stealthily opened the door.

All was closed and quiet. Her flesh tingled. Her nose flared. The sheets were pulled over the pillows and tucked neatly into the mattress. The mosquito netting was tied into a hanging bundle, as if no one had slept there at all.

She picked up a woman's bracelet from the table. Fingering the colorful beads, she pictured the stranger. She was black as night with dark, almond eyes and white, even teeth. She had striking cheek-bones. She loved to dance and was wonderful in bed.

Did she help with chores? Kwassi criticized Ruth's housekeeping, mocking her half-hearted attempts to sweep and scrub. He wouldn't touch her during her period. There was so much she didn't understand; how had they ever become so involved? Would he buy this woman a necklace? She placed her key next to the bracelet. Her heart sank to the ground as she softly locked his door behind her.

≥15≤

After waiting and waiting the *mille kilos* was at last en route north to Korhogo. By siesta time the rich forest had thinned into yellow savanna and scrubby trees. Humidity evaporated into dry air that hinted of desert and left grit on the skin. When the sun went down the tarp was unrolled to cover the windows. Africans huddled together in cotton wraps as Ruth shivered alone under a caked layer of dust and sweat.

She got out the hand-drawn map Randy had sent her. In daylight she could make a taxi driver understand where to go, but it was already too dark, and her mind refused to make a plan. She kept imagining hundreds of different endings to her story. In all of them Kwassi begged her to come back and stay forever.

The motor died about thirty kilometers from Korhogo. There were blank faces and excited voices from the stranded passengers. Ruth closed her eyes and vowed to make sure that Kwassi would never forget her. An hour later when head lights flashed, most of the travelers rushed from their seats and squeezed into the *mille kilos* stopped beside them. She stayed behind with a small group of Upper Voltans who had slept through the whole thing.

When Ruth finally reached Korhogo after midnight the town was tomb dark. Pocket flashlights, the only light source, did little to illuminate her thoughts. It's almost Christmas, she remembered suddenly. Snow storms, fireplace chats, hot apple cider, midnight mass, and cross-country skiing seemed like relics from another life.

"*Vous cherchez, Madame?*" A black face detached from shadows.

"*Oui.*"

"*C'est tard,*" he said. "*Je te trouverai une chambre, ma fille.*"

He swung her suitcase up on top of his head, and she followed without hesitation. He drove her to a small, low building that resembled a gas station, unlocked a door, and went away.

Ruth walked across the sandy floor and washed her face in a tiny, cracked sink. She undressed, put aside a man's clothing strewn across the bed, and slowly settled under tattered sheets. A loud knock interrupted her calm.

She opened the door a crack. *Monsieur* was back with half a loaf of French bread and a bottle of beer.

"*Voilà. Bon appetit.*"

They bid each other good night, and he was gone.

Ruth swallowed the stale bread and felt it catch in her throat. She twisted open the bottle and took a swig. The beer ran down her throat like a mountain stream, pushing the gummy mass painfully into her stomach. She set the food on the floor and climbed back into the dirty bed. Her last thoughts were of Kwassi, as the bread swelled like a sponge, filling her emptiness.

Ruth slept soundly until dawn when she floated in and out of sunrays, preferring to doze for a while longer. Later she was aware of a noise, perhaps a dream. The door was opening, and a man was entering. She opened her eyes a crack and concentrated on breathing deeply. She was good at ignoring people. He went into the bathroom.

The shower stopped before she had decided what to do. She turned her face to the wall, curled into a ball, and held her breath as she feigned sleep. She listened to footsteps and the rustle of clothes. Finally the door opened and closed. She was alone again.

Ruth flung back the sheets and threw on her soiled clothes. She washed her face, secured her braid, picked up her suitcase, and stepped out the door.

"Mademoiselle, as-tu bien dormi?" Her faithful scout was back. Did he really want to help? Or did he want something else?

"Oui, très bien, merci." She smoothed out the crumpled map and asked if Randy's house was far away.

He knew exactly where he was going, driving down a long dirt road until he stopped at a white villa on the outskirts of town. It looked like a place Randy would like, spacious and clean with a wrought iron fence. She thanked him profusely and pressed several francs into his palm as she shook hands good-bye.

≥16≤

The Americans were in a mood for a hike so after siesta they decided to show Ruth Mount Korhogo. They walked the open savanna in single file, lost in tall grasses that bowed to the sky. They looked like tourists on a safari in straw hats, shorts, T-shirts, and walking shoes. Ruth was the exception. Her red sunglasses, halter sundress, and sandals seemed more appropriate for a French cocktail party.

After a while they passed through a tree grove. When they came upon clay huts huddled in thick, green shadows, they all paused awed by a sense of mysterious taboo.

"The Poro initiation rites," Randy whispered.

"Here?"

"Yeah, you know. How boys become men."

"I didn't know Ivorians were circumcised," giggled Carol, a plump 24-year-old home economics major from Los Angeles.

"Bet Ruth does," Elaine commented.

"Hush up!"

"Women as well as men," Ruth answered as she tentatively touched her camera and then moved softly on.

They relied on snapping twigs and rustling grass to keep track of each other in the dense foliage and came together again in a clearing at the foot of Mount Korhogo. From there they climbed a path that disappeared into a stream. They waded through currents and pebbles, grabbing branches for balance and then collapsed into a heap on the shore. Ruth massaged her sore feet and snapped a few photos.

"Ruth wins first prize for best-dressed P. C. volunteer," Elaine stated.

"This is the way we dress at home. In Adzopé, I mean."

"Wow, you're kidding," Carol said. "You always wear a dress? What's it like there? Any cute French teachers?"

"I haven't met any. I'm thinking of moving."

"Moving?" Randy asked. "To a different house?"

"No, to a different town. Someplace with a pool closer to Abidjan."

"Anywhere farther from Leslie would be an improvement," Paul agreed.

"They'll never finish the swimming pool at the hotel," Ruth sighed. "I've got to have more water. I'm dying of boredom. Besides, I don't think they like me very well."

"Who?"

"The people in Adzopé. They know where I am all the time."

"It's the tom-toms," Paul explained. "Instead of telephones they use drums."

"It's incredible. It's like they have telepathy. This guy, Adé, showed up at school one day out of nowhere looking for me. I don't know how he knew I was there."

"I don't think it's so surprising," Randy commented. "After all, we're in a country of masked gods."

"I'm so sick of women banging on tin cans," Elaine complained. "They're still in the stone age as far as I can see."

"Sometimes it's hard to live here," Ruth agreed. Often men stared as she walked by, hissing at her like a snake. At first she thought it was because they found her vulgar or offensive. But after awhile she decided that no one, not even Ivorian males, could possibly be so rude, so she had stopped taking it personally. Perhaps they were merely trying to get her attention.

"What do you do for fun?" Carol asked.

"Read, write, visit Leslie."

"I cruise on my mobylette into the peanut fields." Paul ran his fingers through his hair, now mid-length and squinted at Ruth. "Reminds me of Viet Nam. Sometimes I even catch myself slowing down, scanning the ditches, waiting for something to move," he confided. "Like I'm on patrol again. I guess it's a reflex."

"I run in the jungle at night," Ruth filled in the awkward silence, embarrassed for Paul. Although he was not popular with the other volunteers, he seemed vulnerable to her. She took off her sunglasses and polished them with her skirt.

The last time she had gone for a ride the cops had been hovering around the intersection of *rue du Président* just outside Adzopé, smoking and chewing cola nuts, their paddy wagon parked off to the side. That day they had not stopped her, but they had watched her every move as she whizzed by in her red dress, blue sandals, and yellow helmet.

...

Ruth leaned forward, forcing herself up and up on the narrow path, believing the end was in sight. Grasping bushes, she steadied her weight as stones rained below. Her eyelids throbbed. She wished she didn't have to wear contact lenses. She wished she had brought tennis shoes. She wished Kwassi were here to massage her feet, his fingers traveling every channel and tributary on her sole. He said he could read feet, just like a palm. She had never believed him until now. Now she knew she could not live without him.

At last she straightened her back, stepped up onto the summit, and saw Korhogo at her feet. Her friends joined her, one by one, huffing and puffing, shouting with delight. They stretched their legs and backs, sat down on the rocks, and passed around a joint.

"Can you believe we're here? That we're really in the Peace Corps?"

"It's a lot better than Vietnam."

"If the world only knew!"

"Speak for yourself!"

"Ruth, what do you see in Kwassi anyway?" Elaine asked. "Are you doing it because we were advised to be friendly with the natives?"

"Doing what?"

"I didn't know you were seeing him!" Carol was surprised.

"I'm not," Ruth replied dreamily. "I'm seeing the sky. Far out."

The volunteers gazed above, distracted by giant puff balls in powder blue.

"Look at that!"

"Where?"

"Up there," Ruth pointed to a cloud. "Can't you see it?"

"I don't see anything but a bird." A black vulture made a dive and disappeared into a clump of scraggly trees.

"There's dead meat here," Paul stated. "I can smell it."

"I want to hear about Kwassi. Are you seeing him or not?" Carol demanded.

"I was." Ruth was still looking at the clouds. "But now I don't know. I think he has other girlfriends."

"You are *so* naïve." Elaine was an authority. "Ivorian men fuck around all the time. You're only one of his many."

"Stop picking on her!"

"Are you a Republican?" Paul's eyes narrowed as he focused on Ruth. "Did you vote for Nixon?"

"I think you should dump him," Elaine said. "Before you pick up something really nasty."

"You're on the pill, aren't you?" In Carol's view, pharmaceuticals solved everything.

"I think we should throw Ruth off the cliff." Randy jumped to his feet, itching to liven up the party and divert the conversation away from Kwassi.

"Why? What have I done?"

"Something's gotten into you. You're deluded. Crazy."

"Yeah, Kwassi's just after your body," Carol agreed.

"Your uncircumcised *white* body," Elaine added. "European wives *are* a status symbol you know."

Randy dragged Ruth to the steep slope, tickling her ribs as he threatened to push her over the edge.

"Don't make me laugh!" she gasped.

"Little dreamer! You need to be awakened, if rudely! What are your last words?"

"Stop! Stop!" Ruth howled, laughing out of control. "Ouch! My foot!"

"This pot is almost as good as we had in 'Nam." Paul slowly got out his binoculars to search for feasting vultures beyond the cliff.

The volunteers in Korhogo had spacious homes, cooking utensils, canned food, and a huge paperback library. They had *aperitifs* every afternoon, obedient houseboys, parties with the French, a record player, and a small, concrete swimming pool. In the mornings they took a taxi to the open-air market, past well-kept villas and Sénoufo shepherds herding bony cattle. They shopped for tie-dyed T-shirts and boldly-printed fabric. Ruth bought a carved Yacouba mask that had Kwassi's brooding eyes. At noon Randy served cold beer and stuffed avocados. During siesta Ruth basked in the breeze of the north bedroom hammock.

On Christmas day they feasted on rice and sauce, roast chicken, baked squash, fried yams, chocolate chip cookies, and drank huge quantities of cheap French wine. The meal went on for hours, enhanced by cigarettes and African pot.

After dinner Randy got out an old, decorative blade that

looked like a dagger. He circled the table with a *Côte d'or* chocolate bar, placing two squares in each mouth.

"Suck, don't bite," he commanded. He took his place at the head of the table and pointed his knife at Elaine. "Stick out your tongue and show me. Anyone who bites instead of sucks gets cut."

"Is this your version of the Poro initiation?"

"Isn't chocolate supposed to be a substitute for sex?"

"It isn't, *believe* me."

One by one, Elaine, Carol, and Paul opened their mouths to display the brown melting goo. But when Ruth stuck out her tongue, the chocolate was broken in two.

"I can't look," Paul covered his eyes. "I'll have a flashback to Phnom Phen."

"She won't be able to French kiss anymore," Carol giggled.

Ruth groaned. Her stomach, accustomed to yogurt and fruit, was full of concrete. It would take forever to digest Christmas dinner. She blew a kiss to Randy's menacing knife and made her way to the kitchen where she took a glass from the cupboard and filled it from the tap, ignoring Randy's protests that it was unfit to drink. After clearing the dishes, Randy plugged in the record player. They skinny dipped in his stagnant pool and danced to Gloria Gaynor all night long.

. . .

A few mornings later Ruth hugged Randy good-bye and boarded the train for Abidjan. He told her the train would be more comfortable than a *mille kilos*, even though it was not air conditioned and there weren't enough seats. She was surprised to find a bar and a restaurant inside, although it was too hot and crowded to eat or drink. Ruth was glad for the restrooms. They were filthy and there was no water, but it was better than asking a *mille kilos* driver to stop so she could pee on the roadside.

Delays were numerous on the single track that connected the desert to the jungle. As they waited on sidetracks, heads of calabashes passed under the windows: yams and kola nuts in the morning, pineapples and papayas in the afternoon. The aisles in first class were blocked with passengers' belongings long before noon. By evening second class was a garbage dump of banana peels, newspapers, pots and pans, and babies. Ruth ended up standing in the space between cars.

It was dark when she reached Abidjan. Kwassi's bedroom shutters were closed. She lifted her hand to knock, but turned the doorknob instead and slipped in quietly. He was in the courtyard, listening to the news on BBC radio.

"How was Korhogo?"

"Fine. I'm tired. How was. . . Did you have a good time?"

"Yes. But I spent so much money. I'm broke."

She undressed, took a shower, and settled into his bed.

After a while the man she had sworn she would never go back to was finally beside her. She lay there silently and waited for him to touch her first.

≥18≤

Kwassi had missed Ruth over the holidays, fearing he had lost her forever. He recognized the irony. During his student days he had been a fervent political activist, criticizing President Houphouët-Boigny for his courtship of the French, scorning bourgeois signs of success. No plush furniture, champagne, or video cassettes *chez lui*! For awhile he had even considered a degree in law, eager to champion The Cause: it was time to shed the shackles of colonial imperialism and preserve Ivorian traditions. There was much work to do. Many employers preferred to hire even incompetent French before an educated Ivorian. These expatriates so warmly embraced by the President not only took away jobs, but lived in luxury and avoided mixing with the natives. In addition, *la conjoncture*, world recession, was having a negative impact on business. President Houphouët-

Boigny was again to blame, in Kwassi's opinion, for having followed colonial models. Now they had to pay the price. The glut of coffee in the world market had been followed by a huge drop in the price. Coffee profits, normally part of the Ivorian government budget, had disappeared, which meant less money for roads, schools, and health care. Everywhere he witnessed the decay of the Ivorian cultural foundation, due to consumerism and dependence upon the West.

But this American had swept him off his feet. He knew he should do everything he could to discourage their deepening relationship. Although marriage was impossible, he couldn't control his feelings. She made him crazy and reckless in every respect. At times she was like the warrior, *ezali danto,* running for miles and swimming like a serpent. She could be as innocent as a child then, as sudden as a cloudburst, become tough and stubborn. Most often she was warm and passionate, possessed by *ezile freda,* the female spirit of love. He would drop everything for her totems of mirrors, shells, and flowers. They delighted in each other's secrets, their passionate sea of pleasures. He was sure she regarded him as uncivilized, primitive, maybe even savage in some ways. Yet she was not afraid. On the contrary, she tamed him as a wild tiger. What would happen next? Out of remorse and fear he presented her with a golden bracelet inscribed with a Baoulé proverb: "True love, like a foreign land, once visited is never forgotten."

...

"What would *your* people think?" Kwassi lamented, trying to explain his predicament to her the next day. "Two people like us—" They stood side by side, evaluating their reflection in Kwassi's cracked mirror above the little courtyard sink.

"I'd make them understand. Besides, there are mixed couples everywhere in Abidjan. It's not unusual. European wives are a symbol of success for some Africans."

"My dream lover," Kwassi kissed her neck. "I shall have you made into my spouse of the otherworld."

"What's that?"

"The Abidjis believe we each have a mate left behind at birth who is rejoined with us in death."

That night their lovemaking was frantic, as if panic had entered their lives.

...

Ruth strapped on new, plastic high heels and practiced walking. Tall and elegant, she hoped Kwassi would notice. They were going shopping together, a rare pleasure since Bouaké. They boarded a bus and got off at the downtown market, a wide expanse of wooden stalls under thatched roofs.

"I want to look at the ivory."

"*Toobaboo! Toobaboo!*" Children swarmed and shouted, hands stretched out for money.

Kwassi shooed them away, and Ruth turned to admire huge elephant tusks delicately carved into fanciful designs.

"I should at least buy some of this since I'm in the Ivory Coast. But I don't like to think of the poor animals."

"You have yourselves to thank for that. We kill elephants for tourists."

"I'm not a tourist," she retorted.

She spoke with the vendor about an ivory pendant. He lowered his price a bit. She moved away, and he called her back. The serious bargaining began.

"*Ma belle.* This will be lovely around your neck."

"Perhaps you'll throw in a ring to match."

They haggled and finally settled. The vendor wrapped the ivory crescent in a newspaper, and Ruth dropped the package into her purse.

"How'd I do?" she asked Kwassi.

"You paid too much. But it's only fitting that you should."

‡19‡

Ruth returned to Adzopé and her duties at the school. There were days she couldn't stand the routine and hovered on the edge of morose madness. She would sit on her back step and pass away the dull hours, listening to stray cats howling. At other times she was consumed by a fever that burned her to the bone. At these moments she went to bed and read Russian paperback novels of snowstorms and blizzards. Ultimately, there was only one cure. She waited day after day until she and Kwassi were together again.

...

In Ruth's tiny kitchen dirty dishes were piled in the sink and stacked on the counter, littered with puddles of tomato sauce and fish skeletons, pineapple rinds and papaya seeds.

"Mamadou says it's a feud," Ruth explained to Kwassi. "Something about the new electric plant."

"Mamadou knows," Kwassi said. He stood framed in the

blue front door, travel bag over shoulder, clothes wrinkled and dirty, steaming with sweat. "But this is nothing."

"Nothing! It's the third day in a row that we've been without water and electricity!"

"The Foula want to construct a new electric plant on the Abidji burial grounds, and for that reason there is trouble. But this is not new. We've been fighting for centuries."

"I don't get it."

"Adzopé needs more electricity for the new hotel and the cultural center."

"A cultural center? It'll take forever to build. Why bother?"

"To attract tourists."

"Tourism? In Adzopé? You're kidding. This place is a dump."

"Modern ideas bring change and discord. It's a pity. Don't you have water set aside?"

"Well, no." Ruth's voice trailed off sheepishly. "I've been drinking tap water all this time."

"You're not sick?"

"Never. But I'm gaining weight." She figured she had put on about five pounds during the past few months. That probably explained why she was so lethargic. Her body felt like an iron weight sinking into the core of the earth.

"You're still my *petite américaine.*" Kwassi gave Ruth a quick kiss.

...

"The Ivorians would be lost, totally, without the French and Americans. Or any white people for that matter," Leslie added, lighting another candle at Ruth's dinner table that evening.

"What makes you say that?" Kwassi asked.

"Look how disorganized they are! They're never on time. Never able to do things logically and coherently. Look how long it's taking to complete the new hotel! If you want anything accomplished, you have to first give them money."

"That's a generalization," Ruth said, trying to be tactful. "Not everyone, of course."

"I mean everyone." Leslie stated firmly. "Ivorian men are the worst."

"What's your standard?" Kwassi countered. "The American white male? Why should he be a role model for us?"

"Males are not the best role models," Leslie admitted. "But here they're even worse. My school director keeps sleeping with the female students. It's disgusting."

"It's perfectly acceptable here."

"It's *very* shocking."

"Why? Don't you come from the country of free love?"

"These are only girls, fifteen, sixteen years old. Some of them get pregnant." Ruth hated taking sides, but she agreed with Leslie. She got up from the table and disappeared into the kitchen to fetch more wine.

"Men are vultures," Leslie said shrilly. "I'm so sick of it. They stare like they can't wait to get their hands on me."

"That might not be a bad idea," Kwassi said wryly. "How long has it been since you've had a good fuck? Don't get me wrong," Kwassi continued, "I'm not volunteering. But Mamadou might be interested."

Leslie threw down her fork, grabbed her bag, and stomped out.

"I've never seen her so upset," Ruth sighed, returning to her chair at the table. "Now what?"

Kwassi picked up a wishbone from his plate and held it out to Ruth. She closed her eyes, paused a moment, then snapped off her end to win a silent wish.

Later Ruth and Kwassi sat opposite each other in the dim living room. Ruth held a pocket flashlight, throwing spotlights on lizards playing tag across the blue stucco wall.

"Capitalism is responsible for the world's ills. We've been raped by the West."

"Why did you go to study and live in England? Why did you learn English?"

"One must fight the enemy with his own weapons."

Ruth shut the flashlight off to hide the impatience on her face.

"Am I your enemy?" she asked. She had voted for McGovern and worshiped Betty Friedan.

"For some," Kwassi replied. "For example, marriages outside my tribe are taboo. One of my uncle's roles is to preserve the purity of our ways."

"Your uncle?"

"He's the elder of our tribe, now that my father has passed into the spirit world."

"It seems everyone's related here," Ruth observed.

"Except you and me. We are as different as night and day. Yet, you are my only love. That is my problem, a fundamental paradox. I wish I could have you forever. But I cannot. You belong to your people. And I to mine."

Lying beside him that night, Ruth recalled Kwassi's words and wondered if he really loved her. He kept pushing her back with hurtful allegations and judgments. Yet, each time he would make amends and consume her with a fervor that seemed to grow with each little argument. She wanted to hold him, but it was too hot. Besides, he was already sleeping, and she knew he would not like being disturbed.

20

Kwassi returned to Abidjan the next morning, advising Ruth to leave the taps open just in case water returned. After he left she drank a soda, sponged off with Evian water and a few hours later faced her class with an empty stomach and a carefully memorized speech.

"Good morning, class. As you know, we will calculate grades today. I will call your name and give your test scores. Add them, divide them by three. Then compare your average with mine."

"*Comment! Qu'est-ce qu'elle dit? En anglais? Ça ne va pas non!*"

"Be quiet, class!" She commanded sharply, waiting for the noise to subside.

"We always do it together on the blackboard, Miss," her best student finally offered. "In French, please."

She had never been able to do math in public, let alone in

French. Her procedure had to be followed.

White teeth glittered in a black ocean as tides of sticky air washed though the classroom. Stoically she went down the roster, naming each student, stating each average. Her tongue seemed thick as cotton as she stumbled over the words. The students giggled and mimicked her accent, louder and louder, until Kouamé jumped over a desk. At that moment Mr. N'Guessan suddenly appeared in the doorway. In a flash the students were shocked into silence.

"Miss Sawyer, such a disturbance! I thought there was no teacher!" The Director left as quickly as he had arrived and the class went wild. Infuriated, Ruth picked up her English books and slammed them down on the desk with all her might. Finally she had their attention.

"This is it," she told them. "You all get an `F' for your grade in conduct."

"Miss, Miss!" they cried as she turned on her heel and headed for the door. "Come back!"

Ruth marched forward without a backward glance. She hated looking a fool, especially at school.

By the time she reached home her hands had stopped trembling, although her heart was still throbbing and she was close to tears. Everything seemed wrong. But when she discovered brown, rusty liquid chugging noisily from the kitchen faucet, the urge to weep evaporated. Soon she would drink again.

...

Leslie was not having a good day either. She stood near her front steps, attempting to inflate her flat mobylette tire with a small metal pump. Several little African boys playing mankala with pebbles in the street stopped to stare at the white woman huffing and puffing, working up a sweat. Frustrated, after several minutes she threw down the useless pump.

"Fuckin' piece of shit! Government surplus!"

A shadow fell upon her and she looked up to see Mamadou. "May I assist you?" he inquired.

Leslie sighed and held out the pump. "I can't get the hang of this."

"What can you expect? Riding a man's machine!" He still wasn't used to Ruth and Leslie roaring down the street, legs spread and hair flying. He couldn't deny it was erotic, but it was hazardous behavior. Ruth, especially, seemed to have trouble controlling her mobylette. He had seen her skid dangerously on numerous occasions. "It's a matter of rhythm," he said, pumping up the tire.

A few hours later Ruth tapped on Leslie's front door hesitantly. The beige stucco house was quiet, the glass windows barely open. Yet, Leslie's mobylette was there, parked off the front steps in its usual place, the pump forgotten in the weeds.

Ruth figured Leslie was probably still angry and didn't want to answer. She had spent several days wondering how she could mend fences after the outburst at dinner. Leslie could carry a grudge forever, and Kwassi didn't give a shit. Still, it was worth a try. She could at least apologize and hope Leslie would forget the whole thing.

"Is *Madame* there?" she called to a young girl sweeping a dirt yard next door.

"Oui. Avec Monsieur."

Puzzled, Ruth pondered the reply. With *Monsieur*? What male visitor could Leslie be entertaining? The house looked deserted. She tiptoed away, smiling with amusement. What had Kwassi said? Maybe Leslie was in a better mood already.

21

In April Hôtel Plaisir was miraculously completed, as Mamadou had promised. Out of thin air concrete mixers and trucks of materials had arrived along with skilled workers and consultants, all of them French and grossly overpaid. Yao watched with distaste, but privately conceded that more tourists might mean more opportunities. Although he hated the French and Americans, he knew they often found it easier to pay him than to decipher the complexities of the village administration. He could make their lives a lot easier by cutting through red tape. All it took were modest sums here and there. A little greasing of the palms. It seemed only fair. Business was business.

The day of the opening festivities, Mamadou, Adé, and the mayor, Mr. Dioullo, proudly stood in front of a crowd of Africans and French on the new concrete steps and cut a red ribbon draped across the banisters. The pool, decked out with parasols and *chaises longues,* was already popular. An African attendant in white shorts and shirt fiddled with his skimming net, pleased as punch with his new job. A few French sunbathed; Leslie read a *Time* magazine article about Jimmy Hoffa's disappearance; Ruth did a perfect swan dive and began swimming laps.

"Americans," one of the French remarked, taking a sip of Perrier as she eyed Ruth in the pool. "Why do they tire themselves so needlessly?"

The ceremony in front concluded with claps and cheers. A banquet would follow in the hotel dining room with much fanfare. It was a great day for Adzopé.

"*Madame!*" the attendant suddenly called out in alarm. Ruth continued her breast stroke, oblivious. The cool, clean water swept through her hair, making her feel like a mermaid. She could tolerate almost anything—searing heat, Kwassi's infidelity, and men hissing in her face if there were enough water to swim in.

"*Madame! Un serpent!*" This time the cry was louder, more insistent. Ruth lifted her head and treaded water near the edge. Without her contact lenses, she was practically blind. Yet something was clearly amiss; Leslie was screaming. Before she could react, the African's hands had hooked under her arms and lifted her out of the water, as gracefully as a ballet dancer. Then he pointed to a slithering, black ribbon in the water.

Swiftly he netted and landed the black mamba on the burning concrete, grabbed his machete, and expertly decapitated the writhing snake. Ruth rummaged in her bag, found her camera, and took a picture. The French made a toast to her narrow escape. Then she eased back into the chlorine blue and finished her mile for the day.

≥22≤

The rainy season came. The sky was gray and cloudy, wetness a part of each day. Huge transparent drops splattered off and on. Sometimes clouds piled up in layers of dark purple and navy blue. The wind swept down, driving palm trees into a crazy, swaying dance. Rain fell in noisy sheets, soaking the already soggy ground into miniature swimming pools.

In the early morning Ruth waited in bed until she glimpsed her students in the road outside her gate, sandals flip-flopping water, newspapers shielding heads. Dressed in frayed bell-bottom jeans and a tie-dyed T-shirt, Ruth removed the bobby pins and let down her waist-length hair. She tossed her head, savoring the coolness, but comfort was fleeting. In a short time the air was hot and heavy again with humidity that rendered matchsticks in her cupboard useless.

Kwassi came to Adzopé often, depending on Ruth to type his master's thesis. They spent hours side by side at her little, portable typewriter. Kwassi said they made a good team. At first Ruth missed her IBM Selectric from college days. But the electricity went off so often, she realized state-of-the-art technology would be useless anyway. Besides, candle light was romantic, and Kwassi confided in her readily when it was dark.

"Listen more often to things than to beings," he advised her. "Those who die never leave. They are in the hut, in the crowd, in the voice of moaning wood."

"That's lovely. Is it a poem?"

"A funeral chant." Kwassi nuzzled closer to Ruth. "The dead are never dead," he whispered.

"What do you mean?"

"We possess the Awanté, the power to communicate with the dead."

"You talk to the dead? How? In their graves?"

"The dead are not underground. They're in the whispering wind, the thickening shade. Everything speaks in the voice of our ancestors."

"Does everyone have this power, the Awanté?"

"No, only our tribe. Women, of course, are excluded."

"Of course."

"Don't worry, my little feminist. Next year I'll take you to my village, Gomon, to celebrate the Festival of the Dipri. The dead are not dead. You'll see."

...

The students gradually quit showing up for class. By the end of May only a few of them were left. Ruth said farewell and wished them a good summer. They would return to their villages and she would stay in Adzopé.

She felt optimistic about life. Kwassi was happy, too. He had finished his studies and would be teaching English in an Abidjan high school in the fall. He would have a new apartment furnished by the government, a big salary, and fringe benefits. He planned to move after his summer military training in Bouaké, required by the government, was completed. They said good-bye to each other tenderly. Kwassi told Ruth he adored her and would miss her terribly. Ruth told Kwassi she loved him now and forever.

...

≥23≤

Yao and Pathé met frequently in Gomon to discuss
the happenings in Adzopé. More and more French were
arriving, technical assistants hired by the town fathers to aid
in development projects including a new highway as well
as the hydro electric plant. There was also talk of building
new luxury housing, some sort of "condominium" which
would place even more power in the hands of a few white
outsiders. The old ways were being discarded more and more
by the influx of foreigners who got drunk at the new hotel
every night. Now there were even traffic jams and plans for
a discothèque.

This Western lifestyle was a perversion encouraged by a few
greedy locals who had sold out, Yao explained. Inwardly, he
seethed at the idea of his influence fading to accommodate
the newcomers. He stood to lose prestige and income
if he didn't maintain his place in the delicate hierarchy of

the little village that was rapidly spreading beyond his control. By this time Yao had transferred his irritation and frustration to Ruth who, in his view, was even more dangerous than Adé, Mamadou, and Mayor Dioullo's plans. The French were liars and cheaters, but the Americans were plunderers. He had instructed his men to watch her closely, especially out of town where she was apt to run. Why would a school teacher take narrow paths into remote villages? Why would she ride around with a camera? Everyone knew the Peace Corps was really the CIA. Clearly she was a capitalist spy.

"I have heard too much foreign tongue since her arrival. She and her twin, Mamadou's friend, have succeeded in corrupting our youth in just a short time," he complained to Pathé.

"Does she continue to sing?"

"Yes. Rock and roll. Her students love it." Yao emphatically shook his head. "We must stop her from distributing cassette tapes. The children take them home and learn the songs."

"Another example of alien values transmitted through imported goods," Pathé agreed. "Have you spoken to her school director?"

"To no avail. He insists that she stay for the next school year."

"Do not be distraught," Pathé calmly advised. "I have directed my power towards her demise. Great pain and suffering are in her future."

"Are you sure she will not escape in time? She moves very quickly."

"Do not worry. She is about to have a great fall."

. . .

Ruth's mobylette landed humming and spinning beside her in the rocky road. Embarrassed, she glanced to see if there were any witnesses. Relieved to see none, she sat up in the deserted trail and straightened her yellow helmet. The candy bars were safe, but raw fish and fruit were squashed in the gravel. She put the chocolate in her bag and stood up awkwardly. With a painful effort she righted the mobylette, mounted, and rode away.

At home she locked the door and cleaned her swollen kneecap with soap and water. She looked in the medicine cabinet, but already knew there were no ointments, disinfectant, or bandages. Little by little they had mysteriously disappeared, along with some of her pots, pans, Kodak film, and cassette tapes. She hadn't worried too much about these petty thefts, nor would she fret about her injury. Everything grows rapidly in the tropics, she reasoned. Surely skin would too.

≳24≲

Ruth looked longingly at the swimming pool and cursed. It had been two weeks since her accident, and she still hadn't healed. She was tired of wiping pus off her leg and shooing away flies from her open wound. She couldn't sleep on her stomach or go swimming.

"Are you going jogging tonight?"

"I don't think so. I'm really beat. I wonder if the natives will miss me."

"Undoubtedly. You're their nightly big event. It's crazy to keep jogging on that knee, though. Why don't you go to the clinic?" Leslie suggested. "They have some French doctors who might be all right. There's also the Catholic mission. The nuns are nurses."

"I'll think about it." Ruth wasn't too keen on experimenting with medical care in Adzopé. "It isn't life threatening."

"These infections can turn nasty, believe me. You might

end up with a big hole in your leg."

Ruth waved aside Leslie's alarmist view. One of her college roommates had been a nursing student. She knew how they liked to exaggerate health problems.

She and Leslie drank Kronenbourg beer until the mosquitoes became too fierce. By then the French had arrived for evening *aperitifs*. They were inside the bar, smoking Gitanes and sipping Pernod. Soon they would be laughing raucously at racist jokes and telling anecdotes about their houseboys, *les petits negrès* they paid a pittance to cook and clean their villas.

At home Ruth lathered and rinsed, wishing the squeaky, clean feeling would last all night instead of just a few hours. She chuckled, recalling the careful makeup and hairdo of only a year ago. If her sorority sisters could see her now! She turned off the water, dried, and carefully peeled away the soiled bandage stuck to the sore.

Tom-toms beating to calypso music kept Ruth awake in the dark. She could hear horns and whistles from the dance club down the road. She raised the mosquito netting, went to the bathroom, and opened the Peace Corps medical kit. According to Leslie, antihistamines were as good as sleeping pills. Ruth popped two capsules into her mouth and went back to bed. It was no use. Her mosquito bites itched mercilessly and her nose was on fire. She told herself not to touch, but after awhile she gave up on self-control and clawed into little, inflamed bumps oozing open upon her skin.

In the morning Ruth's knee was a gooey mess, her insect

bites infected boils, her face a stranger's. Yellowish liquid had trickled out from a crack on her sunburned nose to form a big glob. She recoiled in horror from the mirror, got dressed, and headed for the public clinic on the outskirts of town.

She gave her name to a young African seated behind a folding table under a large thatched roof and went to wait on a wooden bench. She sat, awkwardly cradling her helmet in her lap among nursing women and crying babies. The dirt floor was filled with playing children and vendors marketing their wares on woven blankets. Old men chewed cola nuts and gossiped as a hair dresser set up shop on the spot. Ruth marveled at the dexterity and complexity of her handiwork as she wove shells into a little girl's elaborately plaited hair. When her name was called, Ruth stood and followed the check-in man to a small wooden building. She was ushered into a little room with a folding chair and a make-shift operating table. She sat down and waited again as two Africans in white aprons held down a crying baby to lance a boil on the long, white table.

A door to her right opened and a French doctor beckoned. She sat down in his office and explained in a rush about her knee. He listened, then spoke in long, complicated sentences that she could not comprehend. When he opened the cabinet and took out a long, hypodermic needle she stood up and bolted.

. . .

"Qu'est-ce qui s'est passé?"

"I ran away." Ruth strained to speak louder, but all she

could manage was a weak, breathy voice.

The nuns said nothing as Leslie told them about Ruth's flight from the clinic. They just shook their heads and sighed. Ruth asked them what they were going to do.

"*De l'eau et du savon.*" They held up a bar of soap and a washcloth. "*Puis de l'alcool.*"

They put a cloth to her knee and rubbed, gently dislodging pieces of dried, green pus. Leslie stood behind Ruth's chair, ready to hold her down as the sisters prepared to sterilize her knee. Ruth threw back her head, cursing mightily as Leslie firmly gripped her shoulders. The good sisters continued, ignoring her cries, calmly pressing swabs of rubbing alcohol into the infected wound.

From then on, Ruth took scrupulous care of herself. She disinfected the sores, applied antibacterial lotion, and bandaged. Lesions of mosquito bites gradually disappeared, and her nose returned to normal. The knee took much longer. Little yellow and red dots filled in the open flesh. Then the red dots increased until there were no more yellow ones. These grew into tiny pink bubbles that knitted into new, smooth skin. By the time Ruth visited Kwassi in Bouaké she had only a slight limp and a healthy scar.

. . .

25

Ruth followed Kwassi down a narrow path in a huge field of cacao plants. When they came to a little clearing, Kwassi took off his navy blue military shirt and laid it on the ground for them to sit on and then removed Ruth's sandals to caress her feet.

"I miss you so much. What will I do without you?" Kwassi asked sadly.

"I still have one more year. I could extend my term. I could ask to be transferred to Abidjan my third year."

"You are my life." Kwassi held her foot, admiring her painted toenails.

"We could get married."

"I don't think that is possible."

"Why not? You love me and I love you."

"There are many things you don't understand."

"Teach me. Take me to your village. Let me see how you

live. Let me meet your people."

In response, Kwassi kissed Ruth and untied the bow of her halter dress. He pulled her to him and they embraced.

"Ouch! My knee!"

"Sorry." Kwassi hastily moved. "I wish I could take you to my medicine man."

"Could he really help?"

"We possess the Séké, the power to cure."

"How?"

"The Séképoné applies his lips on the wound and it heals in a minute."

"When can we go? My knee is a lot better, but sometimes it still hurts."

"It is forbidden to reveal this secret to outsiders," Kwassi said remorsefully. "Unfortunately, you must rely upon Western medicine."

26

Yao and Pathé sat on the dirt floor, sipping *bangui* wine from a calabash.

"The site has been cleared," Yao informed Pathé. "They are readying the heavy labor."

"My sources say equipment is on the way."

"This digging is a scar upon our ancients."

"Do not be alarmed," Pathé said calmly. "Wait until they have made holes too deep to dig out of."

"What do you foresee?"

"The great rains will soon arrive."

"Will they drown in their own foolishness?"

"Of course. Once a bird is caught, it's the liver the ants eat first."

...

Mamadou, Adé, and Mayor Dioullo studied long rolls of paper of the hydroelectric plans they had spread upon

Mamadou's wooden table, having first taken the precaution of locking the doors and closing the shuttered windows.

"We must make the most of the dry season and complete the excavation soon. Then the footings can be laid and we can proceed as planned," Mamadou advised.

"When will the bulldozers come?" Adé asked.

"By tomorrow. The delivery will take place at night fall," the Mayor said confidently.

"I have instructed the workers to camouflage and hide them within the forest. Yao is sure to have his spies out in full force," Mamadou stated.

"Will you be able to inspect regularly?" Adé trusted no one after his briefcase had disappeared. Thank the gods for that American woman, the singer who danced through the forest.

"Yes."

"Be cautious. Those Abidji will stop at nothing." The Mayor was used to the rural tribes stirring up trouble, but this time he was determined nothing would be left to chance. Adzopé was on the verge of becoming an economic and tourist center. Nothing would stand in his way of receiving President Houphouët-Boigny's highest achievement award next year.

"You can count on me." Mamadou also envisioned honor and recognition. He was sure to get a promotion, a new car, and more money.

"Soon we will be free from the Abidji and their superstitious chains to the past." Adé rubbed his hands together in gleeful anticipation.

"Sacred grounds, my foot!" Mayor Dioullo scoffed. "Nothing's buried there but old elephant bones!"

The three men chuckled, enjoying their private joke.

27

Rue du Président was a road Ruth had always enjoyed, but lately it seemed different. Where there had been nothing but forest, there was now a hint of activity. Even the smell seemed altered. There was an oily odor that reminded her of fuel. She thought she glimpsed some sort of machinery hidden under the trees far away in the clearing, although she couldn't be sure. The path was being widened, a fact Ruth found puzzling. What good would a four-lane road be out here in the bush? This was not Yamoussoukro, the President's birthplace. She had visited his village during her Peace Corps training and had marveled at the wide boulevards, beautifully landscaped but completely empty. The Hôtel President had a fabulous swimming pool and bar, but few clientele. According to Peace Corps gossip, President Boigny planned to move the capital from Abidjan to Yamoussoukro within the next year or two.

A police whistle jolted Ruth from her thoughts. Ieta and Jola were flagging her down. She hadn't noticed their motor scooters camouflaged under roadside palms. With a sigh she pulled over, dismounted, and took off her helmet as the two officers ambled her way.

"You didn't stop at the stop sign, *Madame*," Ieta announced.

"Yes, I did. You didn't see me."

"No *Madame*, you're wrong. We'll have to take your scooter in. This is a serious offense. We've had a lot of accidents here. People don't stop."

"OK, but I'm staying here with you. See my bad knee? How can I go on without my scooter? If you take it, you also take me."

"What are you doing, riding in these parts anyway?" Ieta asked.

"I need a breath of fresh air."

The policemen wandered back to their vehicles, lit up cigarettes, and smoked as Ruth waited on the road side. This was the Toobaboo Yao had cautioned them about. Maybe they would get a bonus for taking her in personally. On the other hand, they weren't in the mood for any real labor and loading up the mobylette would take some effort.

As they were pondering the situation, a Peugeot came into view. On cue the policemen blew their whistles and the car stopped. Adé opened the car door and got out holding his plastic briefcase and a bottle of *Bangui*. When he saw Ruth, his face lit up immediately. He walked over and shook her hand.

"Miss Sawyer, it is a great pleasure to see you again."

"Thank you. Unfortunately, the police have confiscated my scooter."

"Unbelievable. Wait here, *Madame*. I will attend to this outrageousness!" With much fanfare Adé went over to the two policemen, who eyed him suspiciously.

"Are you crazy?" He asked the men in Baoulé, shaking his briefcase vehemently. "That woman is an ambassador of good will from America."

"How could we know who she is?" Ieta asked. "There's another one who lives up the road here."

"That one is Mamadou's girlfriend," Adé informed them. "You'd best not mess with either one of them. They have the United States government on their side."

Ruth observed from a distance. She couldn't understand a word of the men's conversation, but she figured soon they would light up more cigarettes, open the bottle, and drink. They would slip into French and, after a good discussion, decide what to do with her. Bored, she fished her camera out of her straw bag and took some photos of the landscape: tall grasses, tropical trees and vines, a cleared site in the background. She zoomed in and took several shots of an old bulldozer, partially concealed in the forest. Was it rusted? She couldn't be sure. Maybe Kwassi was right about new construction taking over the village. There were a lot more French than before. The tennis court she and Leslie had joked about had become a real *Club Tennis*. The French had arranged to have a new concrete slab poured, and now they were fixing up *"Le Club House"* for a bar. It would be a true *"Country Club."* Only for French, of course. Possibly an

American or two. The type of company Randy would relish and Kwassi would abhor.

Moments later, the police released Ruth and her scooter. They had had enough distraction from their real duty of watching for Yao's delivery truck full of color televisions. He owed them a cut and there wouldn't be room for this equipment and a mobylette. This woman wasn't a menace anyway. Yao was a crazy thug; everyone knew that. Adé shook Ruth's hand and, glancing at her scarred knee, admonished her to take care.

"The gods are not happy unless one dances unhindered, you know," he said before driving away with a smile.

≥28≤

In August the Peace Corps volunteers met in Abidjan for a
midterm workshop and a physical exam. The new volunteers,
fresh off the plane, were exhausted and in shock. Some of
the women still wore make-up, their faces masks of melted
lipstick and smudged mascara. The old volunteers were
easily recognizable: their faded, tattered clothes were made
of African batiks featuring political statements and revered
heads of state. They spoke French carelessly, using African
slang and accents that didn't conform to college textbooks.
In fact, they had forgotten how to speak entire sentences in
one language, freely mixing French, English, and Baoulé as
they pleased. After one year most of the men looked like
shipwreck survivors with bony frames and ragged beards.
The women, on the other hand, had become voluptuous.
According to the scale in the Peace Corps medical office,
Ruth had indeed gained five pounds. She felt anchored to

the earth, more feminine. Her breasts popped out of her bra; she actually had cleavage and hips.

"You don't look like a Peace Corps Volunteer," Paul commented at lunch. They were at the same table sipping a beer. No one else would listen to him. You don't look like a Viet Nam vet, she thought. His crew cut had grown out over the months into a long, fluffy pony tail.

"What do Peace Corps Volunteers look like?" she asked instead. She sincerely wanted to know, but he never explained.

Ruth was sure she was in good health, yet she was not looking forward to the physical. It wasn't the pap smear that bothered her, although it was obvious Dr. Bob was not a gynecologist. Leslie claimed that as a generalist he was unqualified to do the procedure. She circulated a flier, urging a boycott. Ruth assumed he probably hadn't had much practice and therefore was less than enthusiastic about his role. She had been infatuated with a med student her last two years of college. On their first date he had taken her to the lab to show her his cadaver for the gross anatomy class, a nun who had donated her body to science. He had toyed with Ruth, dating her off and on for a year, then disappeared entirely until one day he showed up jogging behind her on Benton Street. As a marathon runner he had been impressed with her effort:she was the only woman on campus he knew who ran not for training, but for fun. He started calling her again, and finally one night they screwed on the shag carpet of her living room apartment after she had assured him her roommates were gone for the weekend. It was his first time and he came too soon. She hadn't cared. It had taken her forever to get a good night kiss, so even this bad fuck was a miracle. After that, they saw each other regularly and made love every weekend. But she hadn't known ecstasy until Kwassi. How could she have? In retrospect the guys she dated had been incredibly immature, mostly into binge drinking, touch football, and getting laid. They had probably kept score of everything.

Ruth supposed it was the challenge of seduction that had attracted her to Pete. He was cute, rich, intelligent, but also shy and a little boring. Applying to the Peace Corps had been an impulse. He had probably admired her courage, although he never said so. All she knew was that when the brochure came with a photo of a hut in the Ivory Coast on the cover, she couldn't say no. Becoming a doctor's wife would have pleased her parents, but not knowing what she had missed would have driven her crazy. Besides, as she had come to know med students, she realized they were all a bit odd. Nerds. Cold fish. The opposite of Kwassi. Not so long ago Pete had sent her a card, announcing that he had met a nursing student with whom he had a lot in common. She planned to write him a letter of congratulations and good will, but she would never divulge her feelings for Kwassi to anyone back home.

The worst part of the physical was furnishing a stool sample, a feat Ruth knew she would be unable to perform at the clinic. Unlike the other volunteers she never had diarrhea but was frequently constipated, as if a chunk of earth were lodged in her stomach. She requested a take-home bag which she would return the following morning appropriately sealed and labeled.

That evening in Hôtel Abidjan she waited until the bathroom down the long corridor was not in demand. Most of the volunteers had gone out for the evening, delirious with the idea of real entertainment. They could go bowling, ice skating, or dancing. They might even take in a movie, a new release for a change. Some were drawn to the upscale French discos and restaurants while others went to the shanty town streets of Tricheville looking for street bars and prostitutes.

Ruth was looking forward to having the small hotel room to herself. The next day she would finish Peace Corps business and spend the rest of the week at Kwassi's new apartment. If she didn't have a stool sample, she'd be delayed. She had to get her shit together by tomorrow morning.

She locked the door in the toilet and sat down with stationery and pen. It had been ages since she'd written to her parents. More and more she felt she couldn't tell them the truth. They would not approve of what was going on between her and Kwassi and she didn't want them to worry. Still, she needed to communicate more regularly. She decided to fill them in about her stay in Abidjan and began with her trip, which had been somewhat eventful.

"About ten kilometers outside of Adzopé, our bush taxi happened upon a logging truck blocking the route, turned on its side like a wounded animal, entrails of long tree trunks spilled onto the road. It had collided with a Solibri truck filled with bottled drinks. There were stranded vehicles on each side, and

I thought we might have to turn around and return the way we came. Frustrated passengers stood in the road appraising the situation. I felt helpless until we all pitched in and began picking up the debris of broken bottles and shards of glass. Another truck attached a cable to the logging truck and gunned the engine. Black smoke filled the air as the engine screamed like a terrified elephant. The cable went taut and gradually the logger was righted. The crowd clapped, cheered, and opened a few bottles of soda from the Solibra cargo. I took a swig of Fanta orange and passed it on."

Writing accomplished two tasks at once. Ruth left the toilet with her plastic bag filled, and she had a letter to mail home. The next morning she arose at dawn, determined to beat the long lines at the medical center. She stood at the bus stop, the pungent sample carefully labeled, double wrapped in small white plastic bags.

The boy spotted the Toobaboo, an easy target. She was reading a paperback, not paying any attention. Like a vulture he swooped down on Ruth, plucked the white bag from her open purse and disappeared into the bustling market crowd. After a few stunned seconds of disbelief Ruth called out *"Voleur! Voleur!"* A band of school boys hastened to her rescue and galloped after the little thief far ahead, soon to be lost. By that time Ruth was causing a scene, tears streaming down her face, laughing hysterically.

≥29≤

Classes began a few weeks later, and Ruth returned to her routine of the previous year. Mornings were busy with teaching and after siesta she swam at Hôtel Plaisir. In the evenings, when aching for Kwassi overwhelmed her, she put on her shorts and tennis shoes and slipped into the forest to run. The weekends never seemed to come soon enough in the Ivory Coast where all aspects of life crawled at a snail's pace.

When Friday finally arrived, Ruth found Kwassi's new home easily in a modern complex not too far from his old place in Cocody. She climbed the stairs to the second floor and knocked. The door opened, and he kissed her. He took her bag and gave her a tour through the airy apartment.

"This is wonderful! Two bedrooms, a kitchen, a living room!"

"There's even a little balcony."

The white walls were clean and the breeze entered freely through the large, open windows. The black and white tile floor was shiny, the kitchen spotless. There was standard rental furniture, an improvement over the wooden table and folding chairs. Kwassi gave Ruth a key and told her she was queen of the castle.

"How will you get to school to teach?" she asked later when they were lying side by side.

"I'll take the bus for now. I'll be needing a car soon. But I don't have the money to buy one."

"How much do you need? You'll be making quite a bit, won't you?"

"Yes, but ..."

"You just need to budget." Ruth kissed him gently. "I'll lend you some money."

In Adzopé Ruth returned to a dark house which didn't respond to the electric light switch. Another black-out. Yet, there was something else too. Even in the pitch dark Ruth could tell things were wrong. What were her clothes doing here, draped over the living room furniture? Had she gone mad? Was this a dream? She turned on her flashlight and investigated. The drawers and closet doors were open, her affairs in disarray. Why would anyone want her jogging shorts? Her blank cassettes? From now on, she would ask Kofi to guard the house during her absences.

≳30≲

Ruth was pleasantly relaxed after her swim, humming a tune as she zoomed around the corner in her gleaming mobylette. All seemed right in the world on this October afternoon. Even Leslie had been in a good mood at the pool.

The little black body darted out of nowhere. Ruth braked and swerved, almost hitting the boy. His cries pierced siesta calm as he ran to hide. She dismounted and followed him, wanting to apologize and reassure. But the child's shrieks became louder and louder as he cowered farther back into the shadowed doorway, terrified of her touch.

Ruth rode away and parked on her uneven front walk, her mind still paralyzed from the incident. How could she inspire such fear and distrust? She did not realize the mobylette was falling until fifty kilograms of hot metal landed on her foot with a heavy, solid crunch.

Kofi was convinced the mobylette was bewitched and advised his employer accordingly.

"You must take it to my village," he explained. "Our Spirit Master will purify and cleanse the evil spirits. Truly, it is the only way."

"C'est la vie," Ruth shrugged. She wasn't totally against the idea, but it seemed impractical. She could hardly walk.

She had to drive her mobylette the short distance to market for weeks, and when she swam, the pain was so great that she moaned under water. Years later when her parents inquired about the bump on her foot she said "What bump? It's just a scar from a burn."

Ruth effectively blocked out the pain, but she was having difficulty remembering details and waking up from siesta. Sometimes it took her awhile to distinguish dreams from reality. Although she denied her own growing internal disorder, she could not ignore the fact that her yard was fast becoming a jungle out of control. As her possessions disappeared from her house, the plants multiplied in her yard. Where had they come from? She didn't remember all these flowering shrubs and potted plants. It seemed the gods were favoring her, she joked to Kofi. He cautioned her from touching the leaves and flowers and above all she was to wear shoes at all times. No more bare feet, he said, or the worms would rot her flesh. Ruth found this quite amusing until one day she noticed a small red dot near her ankle surrounded by a circle of inflamed skin. Within a week there was a lesion, a running sore which had apparently appeared from nowhere. Kofi insisted it was a spider bite. Ruth remained skeptical, until Leslie informed her that a violin spider could inflict irreparable damage.

"The wounds don't heal. You better go to Abidjan and get some medical care. Don't settle for that worthless Dr. Bob, though." Leslie was still steamed about the pelvic exam. "It was obvious he was incompetent," she insisted. "For a few francs I could have bribed him not to do it at all."

"Why didn't you just say you were having your period?"

"'Cause I need birth control pills and they wouldn't give me more without the exam."

"Why do you need them?" Ruth asked innocently. She remembered her last visit with her family doctor just before leaving for Africa. She had been on the pill for two years and was concerned because her mother had developed blood clots in her legs after a year of use. Ruth had informed Dr. Cruso she planned on giving up the pill.

"Why?" he asked, genuinely puzzled. "Don't you think there are any men in Africa?" He had persuaded her to wait until she got to the Ivory Coast before she made up her mind.

Ruth didn't know how to handle her latest health problem, which worsened over the weeks. She disinfected the sore and kept it clean, but it was not healing shut. Like a volcano, it continued to erupt, discharging streams of thick, putrid pus. She debated whether to bandage the wound shut or leave it open. She wished her college roommate were here to answer. Kofi had the usual advice about relieving the wicked spells he claimed lived in her yard. This was not surprising, as he equated everything with superstition and witchcraft.

He told her the bad spirits lived everywhere and that one had to be constantly vigilant. Once possessed, the only cure was some sort of exorcism. But Ruth's priority was her next vacation: she wasn't going to miss the trip to Kwassi's village for anything. Kofi's job would be to take care of her house and make sure no more of her things were stolen.

≳31≲

"You'll be a big hit at the Dipri Festival tomorrow," Kwassi told Ruth. He stroked her hair, marveling at the golden color framed by the blue of his bedroom window.

"Who will be there?"

"Everyone. All the villagers. And my family, too."

"You never talk about them. Who is your mother? Where are your brothers and sisters?"

"My mother died in childbirth seven years ago. Since I am the eldest, I support my five younger sisters, who still live in the village, until they marry. My cousins, aunts, and uncles are numerous, but you'll see most of them tomorrow. Everyone but my eldest uncle, of course."

"Why not your uncle?"

"He is the Spirit Master of our village. Before him, it was my birth father. Dead for many years, he now speaks through his brother, my uncle. He is a very prestigious man with many powers, including the Awanté and the Séké which is my heritage as son of a Spirit Master."

"This is so complicated. Why can't I see him? Because I'm white? A woman?"

"He must stay in isolation until after the purification ceremonies are completed on the fifth day. By then you will have visited and departed."

Kwassi knew it was out of the question that Ruth stay for the hysteria and self mutilation that would occur later in the week. She would not understand the euphoria of the Séképoné, when men stabbed their bellies like the trunk of a coconut tree only to have the wounds completely closed by nightfall. He had no desire that Ruth meet his uncle, although he realized the Spirit Master would learn eventually of her visit. Pathé knew of everything that happened in the village, as well as in the bush country surrounding it. He would disapprove of Ruth, but there was little danger of a direct confrontation. As oldest son of a Spirit Master and groomed to assume his father's duties, Kwassi felt protected from the old man's legendary wrath. In fact, he was quite popular with villagers who were in awe of his wide travels, education, and his youthful, pleasing demeanor.

Kwassi and Ruth arrived in the evening after an hour's travel by bush taxi along a dusty, jungle road. The village huts, nestled among tall trees, seemed mysterious to Ruth who was a little nervous about her reception in such remoteness. Although she was used to being singled out for her race, sex, and above all, her long, wavy hair now bleached almost white, she felt like an intruder in this simple, sacred place. The villagers gave no sign of discomfort, however. On the contrary, they seemed thrilled by the new face. They greeted Kwassi with tender embraces and Ruth with customary warmth and curiosity. Then they melted away, leaving the couple alone under a thatched roof. Ruth felt enchanted by the small circular structure with a dirt floor and firewood. There were a few blankets and clay jars for water. Kwassi made a fire and left shortly to gather some wild plants.

"I must hurry before the women's exorcism takes place," he said. He explained the women would gather at the village's edge to neutralize the witches' evil spells before the ceremonies the following morning. "It is forbidden for men to leave their huts. We must only whisper."

"Will we be safe?"

"Yes. Actually, the timing is perfect. The Séképoné powers are beginning to approach their zenith." He peeked out the door, then scurried away. Ruth laid her head on a blanket and rested. All this coming and going! She was more and more tired and listless these days, as if her energy were being soaked away. Even love-making she found tedious, a fact Kwassi had taken note of.

"My little Ruth," he had finally moaned. "You are falling into an abyss." Although he had hesitated about taking her to the village festival, he was now convinced he had no other choice. This hole in her ankle was obviously vicious. Her fair skin was growing paler and paler, her life forces seeping away like water in the sand. Her face was tight and drawn, drained of luster. How long had it been since they had gone dancing?

When he returned, they sat quietly sipping *bangui* brought to them by Kwassi's little sister, Dianoune. She giggled self consciously as she entered the hut but was proud of the chance to address their most honored guest.

"Drink it. It's good for you," Kwassi said to Ruth.

"What is it? A secret recipe?"

"Yes, if I reveal this one, I shall die," he said mockingly. He gestured to the open door of the hut where a group of children had gathered to peer inside. "Looks like you're a big hit."

"I feel like I've been here before," Ruth said quietly as the children disappeared, scampering away to prepare for the evening's festivities.

"It's the *bangui*. It opens your mind."

"Maybe my great-great grandfather passed this way once. My mother still has his little wooden missionary box."

"Maybe he was here, preaching and teaching. With his little wooden box and Bible."

"Maybe our ancestors knew each other."

"Maybe. Perhaps he's still here with my people, in the trees that sing, in the grass that sighs."

They paused, and for an instant it seemed the tom-toms ceased and the village was frozen in time. There was only the gentle breeze in the grass and trees.

"Can you imagine us living here?" Kwassi asked.

"We'd have a hut."

"And children."

"How many?"

"Many."

"And how many wives?"

"Many."

"How many loves?"

"Only one, *mon amour.*" Kwassi bent down and kissed Ruth's injury, gently calming her as she cried out in pain. He licked into the open sore, his tongue probing the primordial tissue of the universe as he had so many times before in the dark, secret cave of Ruth's femininity.

Later that night, when the huts were silent, deserted by the women dancing deep in the forest, Kwassi made a plaster of plants, kaolin, and raw eggs and applied it to the infested wound.

"Will this really help?" Ruth was skeptical.

"Remember the Séképoné? It works every time."

That night magic invaded their space, transforming Ruth and Kwassi into primitive spirits locked in ecstasy. Ruth's languor evaporated as Kwassi rocked her in the cradle of his beloved Africa.

In the morning Kwassi removed the poultice from Ruth's foot and assured her she would be able to feast all day and dance all night. The women plaited Ruth's hair with shells and gave her a bright boubou with elaborate embroidery to wear for the festivities. Kwassi donned his tribal robe, the first time Ruth had ever seen him in native costume. They danced, ate, and sang.

. . .

Meanwhile Kofi had taken matters into his own hands. He had been longing for a mobylette for many months, trying to save enough money but not managing, due to his many responsibilities. But now that Ruth was gone and he was in charge, a chance was there before his very eyes. What better way to arrive at the Yam ceremony? The villagers would marvel at his sudden wealth. His family would acquire sure prestige. Besides, the Toobaboo was having so much trouble with this machine, which injured her every time she mounted. He was sure there was a spell, yet he had no fear. This bewitchment was intended only for Ruth, he was certain. Why explain? He had the right to take what was his, and for this week the mobylette was definitely his, as well as her house, possessions, and surrounding yard. Kofi locked Ruth's gate and drove away without a backward glance.

...

Ruth, astounded by her sudden recovery, departed two days later to return to Adzopé. She would have loved to prolong her stay, but Kwassi explained the rites to come were secret and sacred to his tribe. She would not see men who stumbled blindly, oblivious to their surroundings, as women and children writhed on the dusty earth. She would not hear the strident screams and moans, as the good spirit of the Séké entered their bodies. She would not witness the climax of the pandemonium, when Kwassi raised a dagger high above his head and plunged it into his abdomen, nor see him strutting proudly, exhibiting a portion of his gut, as blood trickled onto his white shorts. Ruth had no idea of this collective frenzy, although she had experienced the miraculous Séképoné which empowered Kwassi to heal himself as well as others.

Ruth respected Kwassi's insistence and did not argue. She thanked him for the peek into his enchanted universe and boarded a bush taxi to return to Abidjan. From there she found a *mille kilos* that would drop her off at home.

Near *rue du Président* they came to a halt. The *mille kilos* bubbled and steamed, a pressure cooker stranded under palms. Her seat vibrated like a metal volcano about to erupt. Ruth stood up, swung her legs out the window and jumped, her skirt ballooning into a parachute. There was no explosion, only amusement as black faces laughed at the white woman who had panicked.

...

Ruth arrived at a dim house which again seemed strangely altered since her departure. She couldn't figure out why this should be so. Perhaps the Africans were right about spirits. They were said to be everywhere. Maybe they inhabited her house in her absence. How else could she account for this other-worldly feeling; it was as though her possessions were not her own, as if the house, the yard, everything was transitory. At first she couldn't put her finger on what it was. Then the obvious struck her. The mobylette was gone. She had specifically instructed Kofi to guard it, and now look. Could no one be trusted? Her heart sank as she realized the consequences: she would have to walk everywhere in unbearable heat, take a cab to school, and explain to the Peace Corps. She lit a candle, lost in thought. How could life go from joy to sorrow in just one moment? It was as if in recovering her limbs she was now forced to use them.

Yet, she was not unhappy. As she walked through her shadowed house, she also sensed renewal. A few moments later Kofi zoomed through her gate as if upon a wild stallion, beads flying, boubou fluttering. He rode the mobylette up the front steps and parked it under the window where she had left it three days earlier, an oil trail marking his path.

He was a bit startled, but not apologetic to see Ruth's early return, since he had done his mistress a huge favor in his view. He told her she would be safe now, that the mobylette would no longer torture her with misdemeanors. He couldn't tell if she understood or accepted his explanation. She took a rag from under the sink and cleaned the rearview mirror. Then she told him to polish the chrome until it was shiny as new.

Ruth looked again at her reflection, adjusting her scoop neck-line, smoothing her braids. Why bother? Soon her helmet would undo her hairdo. Riding at night made her nervous; the headlight rattled and shook over crevasses in the dark roads. Cars zipped past her right and left, blinding her to pedestrians who used the streets as sidewalks since there was no other choice. Leslie had fallen not long ago and still had headaches. Ruth sighed and checked her watch one more time, recalling how she had become chorus director for the school program against her will.

"What do they do in the United States?" Monsieur N'Guessan had turned to her during a teachers' meeting a few weeks earlier.

"Ah, la poésie, la chanson, et la danse," she replied, using words that popped into her head.

"*Très bien.* You'll teach the students some songs for the School Program."

There was no piano, no music, only a group of students the school director chose at random to form a chorale. At each practice there seemed to be different faces. She wrote lyrics on the blackboard and the children sang stanza by stanza imitating her voice. Tonight they would sing "Swing Low Sweet Chariot," "Yankee Doodle," and "Yesterday." They were first on the program. It would all be over quickly.

Moussa served rice and sauce to Yao while his mother swept the dirt yard. He hoped Yao had brought presents.

"I enter her house every week through the windows. It's easy," he assured Yao. "Now can I have my magic box?"

"I need the little pictures that come out first," he said. "Photos. Do you know what I mean?"

"Yes, but they aren't very interesting."

"I need them, *all* of them. Next time, search her drawers and hiding places."

"She has a locked trunk. Perhaps they are there."

"A locked trunk," Yao pondered. "Next time ask her what's inside. Maybe you can get her to open it."

"I already asked her. She said it's full of souvenirs."

"Souvenirs!" Yao sneered. "She has probably bought masks and statues, trinkets for the tourists."

"I would really like to have a magic box. And a record player."

"Don't let this white woman fool you. Remember you are your mother's son." Yao caught Moussa's mother's eye as she stirred the big, black pot. It had been many years since they had slept together, yet sometimes he still felt a surge of desire. He wondered if Moussa knew he was the father of his second little sister. No matter. He didn't want to be concerned with paternal obligations. He did enough as it was, stopping from time to time to gossip and deliver a chicken or two. He needed only to wait patiently and soon the Toobaboo would be too ill to stay. Then Pathé would be satisfied and get off his back.

. . .

Kwassi and Pathé stood face to face inside Pathé's hut, too agitated to sit. "She was here in this very village and you did not tell me," he shouted. "You deceived me. Deliberately. What's more, you revealed to her the secrets of the Séké. This is unpardonable."

"She is not a capitalist spy," Kwassi insisted. "She is one of us in many ways."

"How dare you even insinuate such a thing could exist!"

"She is a gentle soul; she has a heart of love. She sings and dances."

"I do not care. She is white. Enough said. Your wife has been chosen. Your first marriage party will be next month. Are you prepared?"

"Master Spirit, I shall obey you in all matters. But my heart is not in my control. Please, I would like a little more time before I wed."

"No! This is what you get for mingling in unknown territories with strange tongues. Nothing but disaster."

"With all respect, dear Uncle, the world is changing. It's for the benefit of our people's future that I have become informed. Educated."

"Forget the foreign land you have visited, as well as this Toobaboo and her corrupt ways."

"I can't."

"Nonsense! Have you forgotten how her people have ravaged our land, destroyed our forests and wildlife?"

"Uncle, I agree that the poachers and loggers have decimated our rich heritage. But the Americans are not involved; it is the French."

"The French, the Americans, I do not care about nationality. They are white, Western, and intent on protecting their own interests, not ours. We must end our dependence upon the outside world."

"Uncle, I fear it is too late for that. We must go on and not nurse old grudges. To pardon an enemy is to break his jaws so that he can no longer bite you."

"Enough! As inheritor of the Séképoné, you must prepare for your duties. Do not dishonor your father by a sullied, unholy union with a foreigner."

"Dear Master Spirit, I promise my obedience. But grant me one request, in memory of my father. Please do not harm Ruth. That is unnecessary, I assure you."

"As long as you continue to see her, I can promise no such thing."

. . .

≳34≲

Ruth stood before her students, wishing they would go away. Like a sponge her body soaked up humidity. She was bloated, weary, and slow. She opened her book, conspicuously signaling the beginning of the lesson. They would do oral readings and write answers to questions at the end of the chapter. Ruth called on a student to read. She listened to the British text about preparing a joint of lamb, wondering if it was comprehensible to anyone in the world.

Mr. N'Guessan was lounging in the doorway, checking on her again. Today, instead of pausing for a moment, he walked into the room. The students stood up sloppily. Ruth stepped aside and leaned against the blackboard.

He sat down at the teacher's desk, and the students plopped back into their seats. Before him lay the class roster on which the student names and grades were printed neatly.

"Kumbali!" the Director barked. "You're close to flunking. We may be sending you back to your village to harvest bananas!" The Director ordered Kumbali's neighbor to give him a knock on the head.

Down the list he went, singling out those with poor grades, ridiculing, and authorizing punishment. The students cried, jeered, and smirked. Despite her dismay, Ruth managed to keep her face neutral.

He saved the smart, lazy students for last. Béatrice, the physician's daughter, got special treatment. The Director personally pulled her black plaits tight, let go abruptly, and boxed her ears. Her soft eyes teared and blinked furiously until they hardened into dark, solid beads.

Randy convinced Ruth to go traveling again during Christmas break. He was going to Ghana. Would she like to come? It would do her good to get out of that hell hole Adzopé. Normally Ruth would have declined, but there was something strange going on with Kwassi these days. Instead of welcoming her with open arms as he used to do, he was silent and distant. Before he had volunteered information, he now withheld it. The last time she visited him he disappeared for the whole evening, explaining he had to visit a family tribunal meeting.

"What's that?" she asked, disappointed at his abrupt departure.

"It's my uncle's cousin. He thinks I've been sleeping with his wife."

"Have you?"

"No, of course not. This is foolishness."

"Why do you even put up with it then? Why bother to go?"

"These are our ways."

Was Kwassi sleeping with others? Ruth couldn't be sure. Not long ago the burning itch in her crotch had been almost as bad as poison ivy. She had raked her pubic hair with her nails and then noticed a dark spot on her fingertip. Peering closely, she had been astonished when the speck suddenly crawled away. In a panic she shaved, soaped, dusted with powder until a week later the lice were gone. But her suspicions did not die so easily. What was Kwassi up to? Did he want to hurt her? These questions seemed awkward, almost inappropriate to bring up before him. It was as if she was supposed to know without asking. But she had no clue.

. . .

Ruth and Randy started out in a *mille kilos* from Korhogo and traveled east. The trip was long and tedious as usual, but otherwise uneventful. The vehicle chugged along, filled to the brim with people, bundles of belongings, and a few chickens. As they crossed the savanna they made a few road stops for food and drink. By now the routine was predictable: the village woman sold rice and sauce, fried plantain, and bananas. There was never any bottled water, only Fanta orange and Coca-Cola that had an aftertaste of refined sugar. Sometimes there was coffee, sweetened with thick, condensed milk from a can. The women nursed their babies and the men chewed cola nuts as the day wore on endlessly under a scorching sun.

The metal seats became more and more unbearable until finally, at dusk, they arrived at a little border town that advertised a luxury hotel with a pool. Without hesitating the Americans agreed that this was the place to stop and checked into a room. Ruth got first dibs on the bathroom. She could hardly wait to wash her face and freshen up a bit before swimming. The firm enamel toilet seat was like heaven. The shower seemed unbelievably modern, until she noticed a dead snake near the drain. She shut the glass sliding door and turned on the taps. Nothing. She flushed the toilet. Nothing.

"There's no water!" she shrieked, barging out of the bathroom, wrapped in a beach towel.

"Don't let this fancy hotel fool you," Randy said calmly. "We're still in Africa." They jumped into the pool, sweaty, dusty, disgusted by their own filth but dying for refreshment.

The next day they continued their journey by train and crashed at a cheap hotel. They slept fitfully on twin beds in the red neon reflection of the "Rooms" sign blinking outside their window. The next morning Ruth claimed there was a hole in the wall where one could peek into the next room.

"Enough of these sleazy hotels," Randy declared.

They decided to take the train to Accra that night, hoping to catch a sleeper car at the last minute. At the station lines were long and disorganized, a surreal procession of Africans who looked like refugees fleeing with their most prized possessions. Ruth followed Randy into the narrow corridor and claimed a bunk, taking care to sleep on top of the sheets instead of crawling inside. They rattled and shook all night through the dark countryside until at dawn they arrived at the bustling capital where English, the official language, was incomprehensible to the two Americans. They resorted to French until their ears became accustomed to the accent. Randy suggested they stop at a corner grocer instead of a bank to change their francs. It was Ruth's first experience of the black market, but Randy knew exactly what he was doing.

"Ghana is bankrupt," he stated. "People are dying for francs and will kill for dollars." They doubled their money and decided to live it up like royalty.

. . .

It would be difficult for Ruth to remember the details of this trip; she was like a sleep walker, overwhelmed by her private anguish. She would wake up in the mornings, her eyes focused on the ceiling fan, turning directly above like a wheel of fortune. The days began slowly as they recovered from indigestion and hangovers. Often they would share a chocolate bar before getting out of bed, idly planning their itinerary. One day they visited Shirley Temple at the American Embassy; one afternoon they went to the beach.

One evening they went to see *Moses* starring Charlton Heston. High on pot, Ruth and Randy laughed at the scratchy movie reel in the outdoor theater until they cried. At some point they attended mass in a grand cathedral but did not take communion. They stopped at the corner photographer's shop and posed for a souvenir portrait. Randy told Ruth a story about a group of volunteers who came to Accra and used up all their money until they had to call home for more.

"They got hooked on drugs and didn't give a shit," Randy said. "Couldn't get motivated and formulate a plan. They lived day to day as long as they could."

"Is that the truth? My parents would kill me."

"That's what I heard," Randy replied. "No kidding. It could happen to us."

As the days wore on, their hotel room became more and more unkempt, and Ruth trailed farther and farther behind Randy, exhausted by heat and sadness. She knew she was losing Kwassi, knew their romance was impossible, knew she would be going back to Wisconsin soon. But she did not want to accept this. She carried her agony, a tight knot in her stomach, and daydreamed, remembering all the bits and pieces of her history with Kwassi, wondering how she could have fallen so deeply for someone so unsuitable.

One afternoon in Adzopé she had been consumed with desire. Craving Kwassi more than chocolate or swimming, she packed a bag and left, even though she would miss the next day of school.

When she arrived at Abidjan, he was not there, nor did he appear until the next morning. He told her that he, too, had been filled with need and in a flash he had decided to drop everything to go to Adzopé. He had spent the night alone in her bed.

≥36≤

Ruth folded and packed her new hand-stitched clothes: a halter dress, skirt, and blouse. The hooks didn't quite match on the dress and the pattern was a little crooked on the skirt, but she was proud of her work nonetheless. She could hardly wait to show Kwassi.

She had returned from Ghana to find a letter from Abidjan along with a *Time* magazine and a package of items she had requested from her parents: contact lens solution, tampons, and film for her camera. Kwassi wrote that he missed her and wished she would visit soon.

She closed her cloth suitcase and zipped it shut. Satisfied, she unzipped it again. She wanted everything neat and fresh for the trip. Tomorrow night she would not be sleeping alone.

She got up just before sunrise and fastened the suitcase to

her mobylette with elastic tie-downs. She would leave her mobylette at Hôtel Plaisir over the weekend and hope no one would tamper with it. From there she could walk and catch the early train.

Smoothly she cruised into the quiet morning air. But as she slowed at the bottom of the hill, she sensed something was wrong. Her suitcase! Vanished!

She braked and turned around to retrace her path. Scanning right and left, she saw nothing. She parked and went to search the ditches. Nothing. The sun was hot on her back, the train whistle blowing.

"How could this be?" Ruth wondered. There was nothing she could do but pack a new suitcase and start over.

...

The harmattan wind howled, flinging back Kwassi's white curtains. She sat on the sofa, his head in her lap.

"Oh my little Ruth! How I shall miss you!" Silently she entwined her fingers into his coarse, black hair, stifling the impulse to yank and pull as Mr. N'Guessan had with her students. She wished Kwassi would stop talking like this. She wasn't gone yet. She had a few more months.

At lunchtime Kwassi drove Ruth through the network of dirt roads, push carts, villagers, and school children. He laid on the horn and screeched around corners. At *Chez Alassanne* he parked, and she quickly got out of his gray Peugeot.

"Well, what do you think?" He asked proudly.

"You drive just like an Ivorian."

A pregnant African woman wrapped in a *pagna,* a colorful

bolt of cloth, came out of the kitchen and handed them paper menus. Ruth used hers to blot the sweat from her neck and forehead.

"How much money do you have?" Kwassi asked.

"Enough."

They ordered. She picked at pink membranes, discovering brains was one food she could not eat. He chewed liver from bamboo skewers.

"Aren't you hungry?" Kwassi asked.

"I'm having more fun watching you."

"It's been awhile since I've had a good meal."

"Why's that?"

"I had to give some money to my uncle."

"Why?"

"He thinks I'm a traitor."

"What have you done?"

"I've been indiscreet. I've transgressed. He's suspicious of you and the things I've told you."

"But you've told me nothing. I've never even seen your uncle. How can this be?"

"One must not question the ancients' wisdom in all things. Soon I must marry."

"This doesn't make any sense. Who will you marry?"

"My cousin, chosen for me by the elders."

"Do you love her? Do you want to marry her?"

"It's the only way he will pardon my sins."

"What does this mean for us?"

"It means good-bye," Kwassi said sorrowfully. "But we must be strong. You have your Peace Corps friends. You have Randy. You've always liked him, haven't you?"

"Randy is like my brother, not my lover. This isn't about Randy, this is about us."

That evening Kwassi walked around the bed and took off his shirt. For a moment Ruth thought he would lie down beside her, but he took a clean shirt from the closet instead. He held his good leather shoes and polished them carefully with a soft, cotton square. He stroked his face to see if he needed to shave and splashed on cologne. Then he checked his money and walked out the door.

That night she packed her bag and left him for good. Again.

. . .

37

She counted, determined to lose five pounds and make time go faster. After the 90th lap she floated, willing her depression to disappear. She would go to the police station one more time to inquire about her lost luggage, take a siesta, and fix a fish. She might even write Randy a letter to tell him she was considering a final trip with him before June when her term would be completed.

At the station she waited, drumming her fingers on the counter. When a uniformed man finally appeared and asked her what was wrong she explained politely, stressing that there would be a reward for anyone who found her suitcase, now missing for almost a month. He disappeared into the back. When he came out again he was holding her colorful canvas suitcase. By now the police had had all the time they wished to examine it, but had found nothing of interest except a few Carol King cassettes.

At home she stripped and climbed under the mosquito net with *The Day of the Jackal*. She visualized clean, cool, pool water, her success at the police station, and the wholesome food she would prepare. She would be happy. Somehow.

Later Ruth wandered into the kitchen, opened the refrigerator, and took a swig from the water bottle. She laid the fish on the white, ceramic counter and gently poked it with a paring knife. Kwassi always ate the eyes. She had tried once.

She cut, hacking and sawing until the head lay detached, eyes staring vacantly. Just like at the market, she thought, where they display the heads because people can't read. So many flies and blood. She cut a jagged line down the belly, scraping out piles of veins. She placed the fish in a blue bowl of clean water, put it back in the refrigerator, and scrubbed off the counter.

In the living room she picked up her French dictionary from the shelf and jumped when a lizard ran out from underneath the broken binding. She sat down on the floor, spread her legs, and began stretching. A knock on the door interrupted her from touching her nose to the floor.

She grabbed a sundress from the door knob, slipped it over her head, and hesitantly approached the silhouette behind the curtained window. Slowly she opened the door a crack.

"*Oui?*" she said, recognizing the policeman from the station.

"I've come for my reward," he smiled and winked.

"Would you like some company?" he continued, moving

his foot forward. Ruth put her hand on his chest, pushed him away, slammed the door, and turned the key. She knew this was probably a big mistake, but she was tired of being harassed.

She removed the fish from the bowl and blotted away the dampness. She poured oil in a frying pan and lit the burner. As the fish sizzled, she set out a real plate and silverware. When it was ready, she arranged her meal on a platter and sat down to eat at the head of the long dining room table.

Carefully she removed needle-sharp bones and put a morsel into her mouth. The flavor was bland, almost tasteless. She got up and fetched a jar of mayonnaise. She thought of protein and roughage, digestion and purging, of self-reliance and discipline. She chewed determinedly, consuming bit by bit the unappetizing food as flies landed on the runway table.

She came upon a black artery in the blood-stained gills while her mouth was still full. After that she could eat no more but absently played with her fork, poking the dead fish on her plate, returning to the past even though she had vowed to forget everything.

...

They were lying close, and he said that she was the love of his life. Then he said some day she would go away.

She said no, never; she loved him with all her might, and she could stay because they would let her teach in Abidjan.

He said *non, jamais,* that one day he would cease to exist because she would have forgotten even his memory.

...

38

Randy and Paul were drinking beer and playing mankala in Elaine's sitting room located on the second floor of an old bank in Sassandra on the southern edge of the Ivory Coast. Outside the big front window was the beach, deserted except for canoes of African fishers who were depositing their catch and repairing their nets.

A knock interrupted the conversation. Elaine opened the door and Ruth stood in the hall, dirty and disheveled from the long journey. Her bleached-out hair fell from a disorderly bun on top of head.

"I didn't think you were coming," Randy said, getting up to help her with her suitcase.

"I changed my mind."

...

Kwassi walked into his bedroom with a load of clean clothes in a laundry basket. He dumped them out onto his bed and began sorting. When he found one of Ruth's sundresses mixed in with his clothes he buried his face in her skirt and wept mightily. It had been weeks and weeks since he had been with her; how had this dress materialized?

...

Randy and Ruth rode double up the jagged coast on Elaine's mobylette. She looked down, visualizing a weightless stomach-through-mouth fall, cracking bones, blood-stained sand and surf.

When they stopped she hopped off clumsily, and the exhaust pipe branded her calf. The burn swelled into a giant blister the size of her palm. She didn't care. Now that Kwassi was gone, she was numb to the world. She swam, daring it to burst in salt water.

"I'm staying on for another year," Randy told Ruth. They sat side by side on beach blankets observing the wild, foamy surf.

"I thought you would." She took her camera from her bag and shot a few pictures of the ocean.

"Here. Let me take some." Randy snapped a few photos of Ruth on the beach in her bright bikini and deep tan. "You look like a California girl," he teased, handing her back the camera. "You never smile anymore. What's up?"

"It's Kwassi. He has to marry someone else. Some child bride for the tribe."

"You feel bad?"

"Heartbroken. I miss him so much. But I don't think I can change things."

"What did you see in him anyway? I never got it."

"It all started with a mankala game." Ruth idly drew circles in the sand, avoiding a direct response. "I guess you're right," she finally sighed. "We have nothing in common aside from memories." Randy reached over and squeezed her hand. She smiled weakly as a jet vapor trailed across the brilliant blue sky.

"Let's swim."

Ruth and Randy stood on red-hot sands, swaying to waves of molten silver. They jumped into sparkling froth and rode the down flow until they bobbed on the other side of the surf. Ruth floated on her back and let the current gently carry her, wishing life could always be so effortless. When it was time to go back to shore, Ruth rolled with the crests. Then the undertow claimed her and flipped her over and over until she was wild. Flung onto the beach, she staggered to her feet, coughing and gasping. As the surf hammered down and seized her again, she recalled that a volunteer had drowned at Grand Bassam a few years earlier.

From out of nowhere Randy's strong hands grabbed her arm and pulled, and for a moment she was torn between land and sea. Then she and Randy scrambled to safety, laughing hysterically.

Randy, Elaine, and Paul sat around a little card table playing mankala and drinking beer.

"She says in Adzopé they follow her everywhere. I told her to take off those damn red sunglasses. Africans think she's a movie star."

"It's that camera she carries everywhere. Doesn't she know it's dangerous?"

"Leslie's staying another year. For Mamadou."

"There must be something in Adzopé's water. Ruth and Leslie have gone way off the deep end."

"Ruth has never boiled and filtered her water. Can you imagine?"

"She'll never get rid of those microbes."

"She'll have Africa in her forever!"

"Who could do it with an African?"

"You're losing the game." Randy went around the board, taking all the pebbles, winning the round.

"The first thing I'm going to do when I get back home is eat barbecue."

"It will be so great to have real ice cubes again!"

A knock on the door interrupted dreams of homecoming.

"What a surprise!" Elaine greeted Kwassi unenthusiastically. Hot, sweaty, and dirty, his car had made the trip in record time.

"Where's my Ruth?"

The volunteers' faces went blank. Suddenly Randy sprang to his feet and shook hands with Kwassi, gesturing for him to take his seat.

"She left yesterday," he explained. "She must be back in Adzopé by now."

"That is unfortunate," Kwassi said, sighing deeply.

"Would you like something to drink?"

"No, thank you. I must be on my way. I must find her at all costs."

When Ruth returned from Sassandra the first thing she did was pull back the curtains and open the windows. She found her bedroom in disarray, clothes strewn on the bed and on the floor. The gold bracelet and market necklace from Kwassi were gone.

Her thoughts returned to the Dipri festival, one of her happiest memories. "Teach me how to dance like your people," she had said the second night as they observed the village dancers in painted faces and beaded hair.

"Each step means something different. That's what makes it so complex." Kwassi bent his left knee and tapped his left heel with his left hand. He shifted his weight suddenly and tapped his right heel with his left hand.

"This is what they are doing. See? This is a joyful dance. But now watch." He bent his right leg and tapped it twice with his right hand, shifted his weight and tapped his left heel with his right hand.

"This is the dance of sorrow. We can alternate back and forth, changing a marriage dance into a funeral dance for example."

"I can hardly tell the difference," Ruth said.

"Exactly."

. . .

He coiled like a snake around her and said that he would bury yams in the ground and after two days eat them so that she would always be his.

She said that she had proven herself, that she could eat and drink even the impure.

He closed her eyes and with his great lips tasted her hidden body, lingering knowingly, and then she devoured him likewise. They moaned and whispered and shrieked in sadness until his hard darkness came down upon her and entered the night.

. . .

Ruth forced herself to pack and prepare for her final departure in a few days. She bid farewell to Hôtel Plaisir, the tarantula on her shower wall, her students, Mamadou, and Leslie. Yao and his force had finally backed off, leaving her in peace.

"You didn't by chance see any thieves at my house?" she asked Moussa one evening. He had shown up on her doorstep, clean and neat, dressed in a bolt of cloth, ready to spend a quiet evening reading a book on her sofa, as was his custom.

"No *Madame*. There's a wedding soon and everyone is preparing for it. There's no time for robbery."

"All my souvenirs have been stolen."

"Your memories? Stolen? How can this be? Do you still have your magic box?"

"Not those kind of memories. My material memories, souvenirs like photos, jewelry, postcards."

"Oh, but that is not important. Unless . . ."

"Unless?"

"Possessions can be used to make spells."

"Spells? Like black magic?"

"Not here, of course, but in the bush."

"Oh yes, I remember now having read about secret societies."

"You have no enemies, *Madame*, therefore do not worry," Moussa hastily assured her.

"Nonetheless, if by chance you or your friends or family find my gold bracelet, could you send it to me? Just put it in this envelope and take it to Leslie. You know who she is, right? The other white woman who lives with Mamadou on *rue d'Ecole*. She'll mail it to me." Ruth gave Moussa a self-addressed stamped envelope. Then she went to the kitchen and returned with a bar of chocolate.

"Don't forget, understand?" She said, giving him the candy.

"*Oui, Madame*. We shall miss you."

. . .

Kwassi wrote her from Abidjan. He told her that he would come in his car and drive her to Abidjan for one last glorious

159

weekend. She decided she would give him the remainder of her belongings before she left forever.

She believed him and waited, but he never came. When she locked her house for the last time it was not empty but amply furnished, more inhabited upon her departure than during her stay.

...

Kwassi drove up to Ruth's house. By that time the windows were closed, the curtains pulled. He knocked on the door, but it was obvious the house was deserted. He sat down on Ruth's front step and took a twig, absently poking a spider mound. A tarantula crawled out of the hole. Kwassi played with it, letting it crawl over his fingers, holding it in his palm.

Moussa spied Kwassi from across the fence and took it upon himself to inform him of Ruth's departure. Dressed in a bright boubou, bracelets, earrings, and shells, for a moment Kwassi thought Moussa was an hallucination.

"When did she leave?" he asked.

"Several days ago."

"Where did you get this?" he asked, noticing Ruth's golden bracelet around his forearm.

"It's from the white lady. For our wedding festival."

"Give it to me. It'll only cause you sorrow."

"How?" Moussa asked suspiciously.

"It will make your heart hollow."

Reluctantly Moussa removed the bracelet from his arm and gave it to Kwassi.

"I'm afraid I've become caught in my own design," Kwassi

said, contemplating the bracelet's empty center. "From now on life will be meaningless."

...

Bulldozers scooped out the red earth into a series of twelve big holes at the construction site near *Rue du Président*. Nearby concrete footings stood in piles, ready to be placed within the holes like stilts.

But the rainy season arrived earlier than usual in a sudden clap of thunder. A day later the construction site was a muddy mess with the twelve holes now filled with boulders like a giant mankala board that had mysteriously appeared to thwart the laying of the stilts. A few bulldozers were grouped at the periphery, rusty and overgrown with jungle underbrush. Within a week the concrete footings were too cracked to use.

Moussa stood on Leslie's doorstep holding the manila envelope filled with Ruth's stolen jewelry. He had enjoyed his secret for a long time, but after Kwassi's words he was afraid the gods would punish instead of reward him for the booty. Leslie nodded and smiled, took the envelope and patted Moussa on the head.

≈40≈

    The airport was festive with French celebrating, going home for another summer vacation, laughing and bringing aboard their own bottles of wine. Ruth couldn't believe she was leaving. Propellers spun, engines roared, and technology tugged. The plane taxied, gathered speed, and suddenly she was light as air.

≳ DISCUSSION TOPICS ≲

1. Although Ruth initially resists Kwassi's amorous advances, she eventually succumbs to his charm. How do you account for her change of heart? How would you define the attraction between them?

2. Discuss the role of the jungle in *Souvenirs*. In what ways do tropical heat and humidity affect the characters' behavior? In what ways does the jungle function as a metaphor?

3. How would you characterize the conflicts that Kwassi experiences as his relationship with Ruth deepens? Is there ever any doubt that he will end up obeying Pathé? How sincere is his love for Ruth?

4. Some of the Peace Corps Volunteers consider Ruth hopelessly naïve about cultural norms in the Ivory Coast. How valid is their assessment of her?

5. References to holes, hollows, circles, and emptiness are sprinkled throughout the story, beginning with the game of mankala. How does this imagery connect to the story?

6. Ruth finds herself in a country where it is often difficult to distinguish between dreams and reality, magic and logic. In what sense does she adapt to this new world? In what ways does she rebel against it?

7. Why do you think there is such an insistence on Ruth's part to jog and swim? In what respect do these activities give her strength? Make her vulnerable?

8. Discuss how memory becomes a narrative thread, beginning with the title, *Souvenirs*. To what degree is remembering highly regarded? To what extent is forgetting equally valuable?

9. The conflict among enemies is part of the plot in *Souvenirs*. In what ways are Kwassi and Ruth their own worst enemies? To what degree are they enemies to each other? If they were to meet outside of the Ivory Coast, would their affair have a better chance of surviving? Why or why not?

10. What do you think will happen to Kwassi after Ruth is gone from the Ivory Coast? What do you think will become of Ruth? Will they ever meet again? What kind of lives will they lead?

Julia Lauer-Chéenne

Julia was born in Kansas and raised in Iowa. Upon earning her B.A. from the University of Iowa in 1974, she joined the Peace Corps and spent the following two years teaching English in the Ivory Coast, Africa. Since then she has pursued studies in French literature and the visual arts. Her photographs, paintings and paper collages have won numerous awards and are part of private collections worldwide.

Printed in the United States
106576LV00002B/25-36/A